A Rat &
A Ransom

Y I Lee

Prejudice is based on fear and inadequate facts.

A Rat & A Ransom is dedicated to a little rat I once owned. She was dear to my heart and became the inspiration for this book.

A Rat & A Ransom

This is a work of fiction. Any resemblance to actual people or places is totally coincidental.

Cover image by the artist Jo Spaul
Cover design by Sue Harrison
Interior artwork by Jo Spaul

ISBN-13: 978-1468145984
ISBN-10: 1468145983

Acknowledgements

A big thank you to my helpful and supportive husband Keith

And a huge thanks to Sue Harrison. Your technical skill and patience made publication possible.

And to David Rhodes, your help with critiquing was invaluable.

And thank you Tommie Lyn for giving me the encouragement to finish the book.

Forward

I had been eagerly awaiting the latest book by Y I Lee. The title alone meant I was keen to read 'A Rat & a Ransom' and I was not disappointed.

Whether read by those age 8 to young teens, or older readers, attracted, like myself, by the title, it is indeed a story which will strike a chord with a majority of readers.

There is tension from the start and we immediately sympathise and identify with Tom regardless of his privileged life.

Tom's desire to have a pet to call his own consumes him. How he eventually has one is an ingenious plot twist.

Y I Lee specialises in subtle allegory and as in her other books, the story is multi-dimensional, with an air of mystery combined with tense and sinister undertones.

The narrative draws the reader in so they become totally immersed in Tom's situation. There are heart-stopping moments of danger and suspense and the unexpected ending stirs emotions.

It is a joy to read a book where rats receive such positive publicity and the authors descriptions of the rat in her book are true to life, with the real understanding which comes from experience, knowledge and accurate observation.

Whilst the book isn't all about rats, it may

help fancy rats to be accepted as the clean, intelligent and loyal pets that they are.

A Rat & A Ransom? – Worth every penny!

Lesley Mackness

Lesley Mackness is a former publicity officer for the Midlands Rat Club. She is a regular contributor and book reviewer for the magazines of the National Fancy Rat Society and the Midlands Rat Club.

Having first kept fancy rats as a teenager, Lesley returned to rat-keeping when she had children of her own with whom to share the joys of rats.

Living in Shropshire with her husband Robin and a mischief of fancy rats and mice, she has had a life-long love of wildlife and writes a monthly wildlife piece for her village magazine.

Chapter 1

Heavy clouds scudded across the darkened sky, unleashing more rain on the already sodden earth.

Tom leaned against the head rest and watched the windscreen wipers. He found their motion strangely hypnotic. He looked away and gazed at the waterlogged countryside flashing past.

His father, Ben, gripped the steering wheel, as he struggled to negotiate the water logged road. He frowned and glanced at his wife. "I suppose with the weather as it is, it would have been wise not to go to church today."

Amy, made no comment, she sat beside him clutching her seat belt and staring anxiously at the road, a frozen expression on her face.

"Don't worry we're nearly home now," Ben quickly added. He peeked at Tom in his rear view mirror. "Are you okay son? How's your sore throat?"

"Alright, I guess."

"That's another reason we shouldn't have gone," said Amy sharply. "Tom didn't look at all well this morning."

"Okay, point taken, but I needed to see the minister so it couldn't be helped."

"Tom could have stayed at home." Amy argued.

"Yes, he could. But you know Alice likes to get on with the lunch on a Sunday. And anyway it's only a sore throat. Isn't that right Tom?"

Tom, smiled faintly, and nodded.

"I hope so," muttered Amy.

Tom had been surprised when his mother told him they were going to church, and to hurry and get ready. Due to the foul weather, and his sore throat, he had hoped to stay home.

He struggled a bit with Sundays, not because he disliked church. Mostly, he enjoyed it. It was afterwards, the remainder of the day. It seemed to go on forever and increased his loneliness.

Tom was the only child of his parents, Ben and Amy Lewis. He was nine. Not particularly tall for his age, but strong and wiry, with large deep blue eyes and a mop of dark wavy hair.

Alice, the housekeeper adored him; he was like a son to her. "You'll break a few hearts when you're older young man." She would say, giving him one of her bear hugs and grinning affectionately at him.

"No, I won't, I don't like girls." Tom's face would flush with embarrassment; he hated it when she teased him about girls. But he loved her and in most cases she could do no wrong, except when she talked about girls.

When Alice was around, the big old house resonated with her laughter. She was in her middle years now, with greying hair and a rapidly expanding midriff, due in part to her love of baking. She enjoyed working for the Lewis's; and over the years had become an indispensible member of the family.

Tom lived a privileged, but rather lonely life. Much of his time spent reading, or sitting in front of his computer. In most cases, if he wanted something, and his parents agreed, he could have it, except the one thing he really wanted—a pet. Tom loved animals and desperately longed for a puppy, but his parents would not allow it.

They were both kept busy with demanding jobs. His father, Ben, was the chairman of a large bank in the town. His mother Amy...elegant and lovely, with her long fair hair, blue eyes, and well-manicured nails, ran a small beauty parlour. They relied heavily upon Alice to look after both Tom and the home. So his repeated request for a pet was met with an emphatic, "no!"

"But I will look after it, I promise."

"Look Tom, Alice has enough to do taking care of us and this house, never mind a puppy as well."

"But she wouldn't have to, I would." But no matter how hard he tried to convince her, his mother's response was always the same. Deep in thought, Tom huddled in his seat and tried to ignore his sore throat.

Rain pounded like a million fists on the

roof of the vehicle as they waited for the ornate gates to open.

Ben frowned and tapped his fingers impatiently on the steering wheel. "I'm sure those gates are getting slower," he grumbled, as the car crunched down the long gravel drive.

The tall avenue of trees swayed in the wind. Ahead of them stood an imposing Victorian house, built of warm red brick. Tall pillars graced the entrance. A well-tended-garden, filled with old fashioned scented roses surrounded the house. Now, due to the heavy rain, most of their petals lay scattered on the ground, reminiscent of colourful confetti. To the rear of the house, a lush green lawn swept down to the river.

Tom liked to stand on the bank and wave at the passing boats.

His mother's voice interrupted his thoughts. "Pass my umbrella, Tom. It's on the seat beside you. I hope this rain stops soon, it's ruining my roses," she complained.

"I think it's set for the day," said Ben, parking the car as close to the front door as he could.

Alice waited by the open door. They dashed in to be greeted by the welcome aroma of Sunday roast.

"Something smells good Alice."

"It won't be ready for half an hour yet, sir."

"No problem." Ben took the Sunday papers from her and made his way to the sitting room.

Tom followed his mother and Alice into the kitchen.

"You look very flushed Tom," said Alice with a hint of concern.

Amy felt his forehead. "You do feel hot son. Why don't you go to your room, I'll come and check on you shortly."

Tom didn't argue, his throat hurt and he felt chilled. Weary, he climbed the stairs to his bedroom on the second floor. Situated at the rear of the house, the room afforded stunning views over the large garden. If he stood on the window seat, he could just glimpse the meandering river. Tom flopped onto the bed, closed his eyes and instantly fell asleep; he had no idea for how long—suddenly, he was awake. Heavy rain pattered loudly against the window.

He yawned and rubbed the sleep from his eyes. Swinging his feet to the floor he perched on the side of the bed and cradled his head in his hands. *It must have been the rain that woke me.*

He went to the window seat, and rubbed the misted glass vigorously with his sleeve. But it was still hard to see. He squinted through the rain, and was surprised to see a black shape in the garden below. Whatever it was appeared to be messing with the gardener's watering can. *Looks like a cat. I wonder what it's doing.* Curious, Tom shot to his feet. Taking the stairs two at a time, he grabbed his rain coat off the hook, raced into the kitchen and made for the back door.

"Where are you going?" shouted his mother. "You'll get wet through, and what about your sore throat?"

"I won't be a minute." He slammed the back door shut at Alice's request, and ran as fast as he could to where he'd seen the black shape.

It was a cat, and whatever was in the watering can had its undivided attention. Nevertheless, it heard him approach and spun round to face him.

Tom skidded to a halt. For a brief moment the boy and the cat stared at each other.

The cat's large green eyes fixed him with a hypnotic stare.

Tom held out his hand and walked slowly towards it, hoping he might be able to stroke it. "Where have you come from?" he said softly, afraid it would run away.

The minute the words left his mouth, the cat hissed...turned, and bolted across the lawn.

"Wait!" cried Tom. "I only want to be friends." Despondent, he watched the cat vanish in the bushes. Wet and fed up, he turned to go indoors, but then he remembered the cat's interest in the watering can. Carefully, he picked it up. *I wonder why the cat found this old can so fascinating.* He peered inside, huddled at the bottom wet and bedraggled was a tiny white creature. Cautiously, Tom put a trembling hand inside and touched it.

Frightened, the tiny creature moved away, but made no attempt to bite him.

Tom caught hold of it as gently as he could; the little thing squeaked in protest. It lay trembling in his hand, cold and soaking wet. Tom could feel its heart beating like a small bird.

He noticed its long bald tail, and decided it must be a mouse. *It can't be a wild one though, because there're brown and this one is white.* He studied it, noting the unusual face marking; a near perfect black mask. Tom knew if he didn't rescue the little mouse, either the cat would return and kill it; or it would die of cold. So as far as he could see, he had no choice. He couldn't leave it outside to die.

Carefully, he wrapped the wet and bedraggled mouse in his jumper "I'm going to take you to my room," he whispered. "You need to be really still and quiet, because my mum hates rodents." With his heart in his mouth, he returned to the kitchen. The room was warm and filled with delicious cooking smells. But his mother's cross expression sent a chill up his spine.

"Look at you!" she grumbled. "You're wet through. Why on earth did you rush out in the pouring rain? You'll make yourself ill."

Tom tried not to panic; he stood frozen on the spot, like a frightened rabbit. Anxious eyes fixed on his mother's face. He knew he couldn't tell her the truth. He tried to think of something, anything, rather than tell her there was a mouse up his jumper. He knew how much she hated small furry things. He prayed the mouse would stay still.

"Well!" enquired his mother, impatiently.

Tom lowered his head, but not before she noticed the red flush to his cheeks.

"What is the matter with you Tom? You know how I hate it when you don't answer me."

He stared at the floor, desperately trying to think of something to say. He felt like the little mouse, trapped, and with no way of escape. "I saw something in the garden," he replied, his bottom lip trembled slightly. He raised his head and stared at his mother. "I wondered what it was, so I went to look." He hoped his explanation would end the questions.

"Why didn't you say so in the first place?" She frowned with impatience. "So, what was it?"

Tom could hear the irritation in her voice. "It was a cat, but it ran away when it saw me."

Exasperated, Amy sighed and brushed a strand of hair away from her face. "A cat, is that all, for goodness sake Tom." Her eyes flashed with annoyance.

Alice stood at the sink washing pots; a slight smile on her face. She knew how frustrating Tom could be when he refused to communicate. She decided to intervene and ease the tension. "Excuse me butting in, Mrs Lewis," she said softly. "But lunch will be ready in ten minutes."

It worked. Amy calmed down and joined her at the sink.

Unsure what to do, Tom stood in the centre of the room, his hand over the tiny bulge that was the mouse in his jumper.

"You heard Alice, young man. Go and tell your father lunch will be ready in ten minutes. And for goodness sake, take off that wet rain coat. We will continue this conversation later." She warned him.

Tom made for the door, grateful for

Alice's intervention. He could hear them discussing him as he hung up his wet coat. Gently he fingered the small roll in his jumper. The mouse stirred. "We'll go to my room in a minute," he whispered. Tom went to the sitting room and knocked softly on the door.

"Yes," enquired his father from the other side of the door.

Tom's hand trembled slightly as he opened it a fraction and peeked in.

"Dad, Alice says lunch will be ready in ten minutes."

His father peered at him over the newspaper. His dark brown eyes twinkled. "Why are you looking so red in the face young man, what have you been up to? Stop hiding behind that door and come here."

Tom's heart sank. A nervous lump rose in his throat as he walked into the room. He wished the ground would open and swallow him.

Chapter 2

Ben smiled slightly as he watched his son approach. Tom's flushed cheeks and sheepish expression was a dead give-away.

"So, what mischief have you been getting into?"

"Nothing," replied Tom staring at the carpet in an effort to avoid eye contact. But to his horror the mouse, now warm and dry, started to move around inside his jumper.

His father's raised eyebrows and quizzical expression did little to ease Tom's sense of foreboding. "Is there something you would like to share with me son?" he asked.

Tom searched his father's face, wondering how he would respond once he knew what was hidden inside his jumper. He attempted to keep the mouse still, while nervously explaining about the cat and the watering can. "I couldn't see what the cat was doing, as my bedroom window was too misty. So I ran into the garden to have a look, but as I came close the cat ran away." Tom paused for breath, aware his father's eyes were glued to the movement inside his jumper.

"I'm listening, Tom, go on." Ben continued to stare at Tom's midriff which appeared to have some sort of alien moving around inside it.

"Well, there's not much more to tell really, I looked inside the watering can and there was this pretty white mouse." Gently, Tom disentangled the mouse from his jumper and held it in his hand.

In a split second, the tiny creature ran up his arm and crouched on his shoulder, where it sat trembling.

"I don't think that's a mouse," said Ben, placing his newspaper on the table and rising from his chair. "That's a rat. Here, let me see it."

Tom quickly scooped the frightened creature off his shoulder and looked closely at it.

"But it is so small, Dad, and it's not brown like a wild one."

Ben took the rat from him. "It's definitely a rat, Tom. There's a lady at church has rats like this. In fact, it could be one of hers." He studied the small animal. "It's young, and, if I am not mistaken, female."

"So, it's not a mouse?" said Tom.

Ben smiled. "No, it's a baby rat."

"Can I keep her dad, can I?" Tom blurted out eagerly.

Ben said nothing. He knew his wife would not be happy. She hated rodents, especially rats. "We'll have to speak to your mother, but you know how she detests rodents, so don't get your hopes up. Even if we let you keep her, you do realise she may die. After all, we have no idea what she's been through, or where she's come from. And anyway, she may belong to Jean the lady at church, in which case you will have to return her." He handed the rat to Tom.

Instantly, the tiny creature scurried onto his shoulder and crouched by his neck.

"Who's Jean?" asked Tom.

"You don't know her, but she keeps a few pet rats and takes them to shows. Weird if you ask me, but I guess it takes all sorts. Anyway, she might be able to help us, and as I say, it could possibly be one of hers."

Tom could tell by his father's voice, he hoped the rat belonged to Jean. His young face fell, and he could hardly hide his disappointment. He held the little rat close to his cheek.

"Mask," he whispered softly.

Ben gave him a stern look. "Now stop right there, don't go naming it. I didn't say you could keep it."

Tom looked at him with tear filled eyes.

Ben smiled sympathetically and ruffled his hair. "I'll do my best son, but I can't promise anything. I need to ring Jean first and then speak to your mother."

Tom followed him into the hall. His heart pounded with nervous anticipation as he waited for his father to ring the rat lady.

"Oh, hi, Jean, it's Ben Lewis here from church. Sorry to bother you, but are you by any chance missing a baby rat? It's a white one with

13

strange facial markings."

Tom listened to the conversation. He could tell by the way his father was talking; none of Jean's rats were missing. Delighted, he struggled to hide his excitement. The little rat sniffed his ear which made him giggle.

Ben put the phone down. "Okay, Tom. It seems this is not one of Jean's rats, but she's coming over to look at it. She says, you will need food, a water bottle, and a cage, but she's happy to lend us one of hers."

"Oh great, does this mean I can keep her?"

"No, I told you before, it doesn't. Jean's going to try and find the rat's owner. If no one is found, you may be able to. However, I can't see your mother agreeing, so I wouldn't bank on it." He went to the kitchen and poked his head round the door.

Amy grinned at him. "Oh good, there you are. Will you carve the meat for us? Lunch is nearly ready."

"Yes, but can I have a quick word with you first?"

Curious, and a little concerned by his expression, Amy followed him into the hall. The next minute the house echoed to a loud scream. "A rat, there's a rat!" Shaking with fear she ran and hid behind her husband. "Ben, what is Tom doing with a rat?"

Frightened by the loud noise, the rat scooted inside Tom's jumper to hide.

"Go to your room, Tom," commanded his father.

"But Dad—"

"Do as I say son."

Dejected, Tom moved slowly towards the stairs.

Hearing the commotion, Alice rushed from the kitchen.

Ben did his best to calm every one. "Hold lunch for at least half an hour, Alice."

"But the vegetables will be over cooked and soggy by then," she protested. "And did I hear the word rat?"

Ben tried to remain patient as he assured her everything was under control.

Alice returned to the kitchen, frowning and muttering with displeasure.

Amy followed Ben into the sitting room. "What's our son doing with a rat?" she asked trembling with anxiety. "You know how I hate rodents."

Ben motioned to a chair. "Sit down dear, and I will try and explain as best I can."

Tom sat on the stairs praying like mad. The rat, warm inside his jumper had gone to sleep.

In the kitchen, Alice used the saucepans to express her annoyance. "What's a rat doing in the house, I'd like to know?" she grumbled. "We should get the pest control people in and get rid of it, nasty creatures! My lunch ruined and because of a pesky rodent."

Tom listened to her complaints and anxiously placed a protective hand over the small bump in his jumper. The rat stirred. "Don't you worry, Mask," he whispered. "The pest man won't get you, or the rat lady. I'll take care of you, I promise. You belong to me."

Chapter 3

Tom sat on the stairs, his elbows propped on his knees, his chin resting in his hands. He could hear his parents talking, his mother sounded upset. He tried to remain positive.

Wrapped inside his jumper the sleepy rat stirred; her soft fur warm against his skin. "I am going to keep you," he said, his young voice full of determination. A loud knock at the front door startled him. He ran and opened it.

It was Jean, the rat lady from church. She stood under the porch light smiling at him. "Hello there, you must be Tom? I'm Jean. May I come in?" She swept past him into the hallway. Emblazoned across the front of her pale blue fleece was a picture of a comical rat.

Tom liked her instantly.

"Okay, young man, where's this rat? Let me have a look at it."

Tom disentangled the sleepy creature from of his jumper and placed it in her hand.

"Well! Well!" she said, looking closely at

the small animal. "You are sweet and what a perfect mask." She turned to Tom. "This variety is called Turpin; any ideas why?" Her brown eyes twinkled with amusement.

Tom grinned. "Is it because she looks like Dick Turpin the highway man, with his black mask?"

"Precisely, well done." she gave him a warm smile.

Ben and Amy heard them talking and came into the hall.

Alice, curious at the sound of voices, stood in the kitchen doorway watching.

Jean turned to Ben. "You seem to have a bit of a mystery going on here."

"You could say that," said Ben with a puzzled frown. "We appreciate you coming over, Jean."

"Oh, it's a pleasure, Mr Lewis."

"Please, call me Ben, and this is my wife Amy. As I explained on the phone, Tom found this rat in our watering can. It seems there was a cat after it."

Jean stroked the little rat. "I wonder where you've come from?" she said softly.

Amy watched her, every muscle tense; ready to run the minute the rat moved. She stood slightly behind Ben, her eyes glued to the rat's tail.

In a way, Jean could understand Amy's anxiety, and did her best to put her at ease. "This is not a wild rat Amy, so you don't need to be afraid."

Amy was not totally convinced; but

18

bravely attempted to control her fear as she held onto Ben. She was aware that Jean kept rats and took them to shows. She grimaced at the thought.

Jean felt somewhat ill-at-ease herself. The Lewis's were relative strangers to her. Yet, here she was in their hallway, discussing a rat of all things! *Life can be strange sometimes*. She thought.

She smiled at Amy. "I would run a mile if this were a wild rat. But it's not, it's what we call a fancy rat, and like a poodle is to a wolf, they have nothing in common. They are delightful creatures and a great pet for a young man like Tom here." She handed the rat to him.

In a flash it ran up his arm and onto his shoulder where it sat and washed itself.

"Oh look! What's she doing?" exclaimed Tom.

Jean smiled. "She's washing, they do it a lot. The fact she sits on you to wash shows she trusts you."

The little rat continued to lick her front paws and meticulously wipe them over her face and ears.

"She's actually rather cute," commented Alice from the safety of kitchen doorway. "And at least she washes behind her ears, unlike a certain person I know." She grinned at Tom.

Normally such a remark would cause Tom to flush with embarrassment. But he was thrilled that Alice seemed to like the rat, and dismissed her dig at his personal hygiene. But he could tell by his mother's worried frown—she was not totally convinced.

Amy could see the rat made Tom happy. But the creature's bald tail made her cringe.

Jean informed them the rat was probably around six weeks old. "I can't understand how a rat as young as this found itself in your watering can. It's a bit of a mystery!"

"It certainly is, so what do you suggest we do now?" asked Ben.

"Well, first things first, she must be hungry and thirsty and in need of a rest. So we'll put her in the cage I've brought. Then if you like, I can take her home with me, while I try and find the owner."

"No!" Tom cried. "Please, let her stay with me. Please, Mother, can she?"

Amy was surprised at his outburst. She had never known him be so passionate about anything before. He was normally such a quiet and studious boy. As she stared at the rat, she had to admit it was quite pretty, so long as she couldn't see its tail. And now she knew it wasn't a wild one, she did feel a little less anxious. But she was torn between her fear of rodents and her desire to please her son. She looked to Ben for help.

He could see the mixed emotions in her eyes. He took her hand and smiled. "Don't worry, it'll be okay," he whispered.

"I hope you're right."

Tom held the little rat close and stared anxiously at his mother, unsure if the look he saw in her eyes was positive or negative.

Amy sighed. "Okay son, the rat can stay,

at least until its owner is found. But don't bring it near me." She gave an involuntary shudder at the thought.

Tom beamed with delight. "Oh thanks mum. But what if the owner can't be found, will I be allowed to keep her then? Please, say yes."

Ben frowned at him. "Don't push it Tom, just be grateful for what you have at this moment." He turned to Jean. "I suggest we fetch the cage."

It was decided they would put the rat in the utility room.

Tom didn't care so long as he could keep his new found friend.

When the cage was ready, they popped her in and watched with interest as she made herself at home.

Tom found a small cardboard box, and with Jean's guidance he cut a hole in it and lined it with soft paper.

The little rat seemed to love it and was soon curled in a ball fast asleep.

Chapter 4

Before she left, Jean assured them she would try to find the rat's owner. "As soon as I hear anything I'll let you know."

Tom frowned, it wasn't what he wanted to hear, but at least he could keep the rat for a while and for that he was grateful.

As Jean's car disappeared down the drive, Alice busied herself serving the lunch.

Normally, Tom enjoyed Sunday lunch, but today he was just too excited.

After the meal, Alice drove into town to see her friend. They had known each other for many years and whenever possible spent most Sunday afternoons together.

Ben retreated to his office; he had paperwork to sort out and a few emails to send.

All the excitement had left Amy with a bit of a headache, so she went upstairs to rest.

Left alone, Tom ran to the utility room carrying a small bit of roast potato. He could see Mask asleep in her box. Gently, he tapped on the bars.

The little rat raised her head and peered at him, her eyes half closed and sleepy. She sniffed the air, her long whiskers twitched—she could smell the potato.

"Come on Mask," encouraged Tom. "This is roast potato, you'll like it."

She had a little stretch and left the box.

Tom opened the door of the cage and held the food for her.

She gave it a good sniff, which made him smile.

"No one is going to poison you, are they? Come on, try it. You'll like it, honest. Alice makes the best roast potatoes in the world."

As if understanding him, she took a tentative nibble, decided she liked it and took the whole piece from him. Carrying it into her box, she held it in her paws and took small bites out of it. Her nose twitched with each chew.

Tom couldn't help but smile, she looked so cute. "Just wait till my friends see you, they'll be so jealous." He watched her for a while, and then ran upstairs to his room. He settled on the window seat and stared into the garden. It was still raining, but not nearly so hard. He could hear the wind whistle as it blew around the house. He leaned against the window pane, listening to the rain patter against the glass.

Usually, Tom struggled with Sunday afternoons; he hated the eerie silence. But not this particular Sunday; downstairs was something he'd always wanted—a pet. She consumed his thoughts; he prayed he would be allowed to keep her. "I hope Jean doesn't find the owner," he whispered. "I know she probably belongs to someone else, but I want to keep her."

In the past when Tom thought of owning a pet, it was always a puppy he wanted. Something like a rat would never have entered his head. Especially as his mother hated and feared rodents so much. But now he wanted nothing else. He had saved her from the cat, and somehow deep inside he knew she was special and she belonged to him.

Tom jumped off the window seat and went to his bed. He lay down and closed his eyes. His throat still hurt and his body felt strangely heavy and tired. *Is this all a dream* he wondered as he fell asleep? He woke to find his mother sitting on the edge of the bed.

"How's your throat?" she asked, concern clearly etched on her face. Gently she placed the back of her hand on his forehead. "You feel a little warm. Here have a drink."

"I'm okay, really." Tom sat up and drank the juice. "I must see if Mask's alright."

"I'm sure she's fine, but under the circumstances I don't think you should be naming her." Amy smiled at Tom's dejected expression. She knew how desperately he wanted a pet, and she wanted her boy to be happy.

Tom gazed at his mother; noticing the strange twinkle in her eyes as she smiled at him. However, her question took him completely by surprise.

"Tom, would you like to keep this rat?" She knew full well what his answer would be.

25

"It's just I've been thinking about it. I know your father doesn't mind either way. So I've decided if it makes you happy and if no one owns it, you can keep it."

Tom stared at her, hardly daring to believe what he'd heard. Tears filled his eyes as he threw himself into her arms. "Oh yes, Mum, I would, it would be the best thing in the world."

She held him close. "Look, darling, it's possible Jean may find the owner of your rat. If she does I'm sure she will let you have one of hers to replace it."

"Oh no, Mum, Mask is mine, she belongs to me. I will be able to keep her, I just know it." His eyes shone as he looked earnestly into her face.

Amy smiled at his confidence. "Okay son, if no one claims the rat, you can keep her."

Overcome with excitement, Tom shot off the bed and ran noisily downstairs and into the utility room.

His father peered round the office door. "What's all the racket about?" he demanded.

"Mother says if Mask doesn't belong to anyone, I can keep her," shouted Tom.

"Oh, is that all, well just keep the noise level down please. I'm trying to work."

"Mask," Tom called as he ran to the cage.

She crouched in the corner of the box, frightened by the noise.

Tom couldn't get his hand in the small hole, so he opened the end and pulled her out. "You belong to me, I just know it," he declared, his voice high pitched with excitement. He held her warm body against his cheek.

She wriggled out of his hands and climbed onto his shoulder. Her whiskers twitched as she sniffed the air. She was not too happy at being disturbed, or his enthusiastic expressions of affection. But to let him know she liked him too, she gave his ear a gentle nibble and decided his hair needed a bit of a trim.

"Tea is ready," shouted Amy from the kitchen.

Tom lifted Mask off his shoulder and returned her to the cage. "I'll see you later." His blue eyes glistened with happiness. "We're going to have great adventures together, you'll see."

Chapter 5

Fred turned the battered green Ford off the road and drove slowly past disused farm buildings. Carefully, he negotiated the ruts and potholes littering the drive and parked the car outside a derelict looking farmhouse. He switched off the engine and surveyed the property. "Well, here we are," he said, enjoying his companions horrified expression.

"You are kidding me—is this it?" Bill released his bulky frame from the seat belt, and stared disdainfully at the building.

"Yep, this is it. It's the best I could find. Home from home, wouldn't you say?" Fred's mouth twisted in an unpleasant grin as he eased his tall skeletal body from the constraints of the small car and walked towards the house. He cast a long shadow in the late afternoon light.

Grumbling to himself, Bill struggled from the car and looked despondently at the run-down farmhouse. "I wouldn't keep a rat in a place like this, never mind a kid."

"Stop moaning, we're not gonna be here that long. Get the stuff out of the boot. There's not much time and a lot to do. After all, we want to make it as comfortable as possible for our young guest, don't we?" he laughed sarcastically.

Bill frowned, his eyes darkened with anger, but he held his tongue. He knew better than to rise to Fred's goading. Muttering to himself he started to unload the car. He didn't like any of this and felt distinctly uneasy. But it was too late now, the ball was rolling and there was no way of stopping it.

He stood by the car a moment to catch his breath and gazed around. *It must be years since anyone lived, or worked here.* The farm had definitely seen better days.

Not far from the house stood a dilapidated old barn. Growing over the rotted wooden frame were thick tendrils of ivy and various climbing plants. The rusty corrugated roof hung on at a decidedly jaunty angle. Without the parasitic plant support, a puff of wind would be enough to send the whole building crashing to the ground.

The house itself was a sorry sight. There were tiles missing from the roof, and a number of windows were broken. Large shards of glass were scattered all over the ground.

Bill noticed a tree branch had managed to force its way through a side window into one of the upstairs rooms. He cursed softly as he closed the car boot. The thought of spending one night in a place like this filled him with anxiety. His heart sank as he grabbed the stuff and made his way towards the house.

Fred was waiting impatiently at the back door. "Get a move on, we haven't got all day. It's not so bad once you get inside." He grinned and led the way into the house.

The strong smell of damp assailed Bill's nostrils, he sniffed in protest. "You sure you couldn't find anywhere better than this?" he grumbled. "And what's that rumbling noise?"

"It's the generator out the back."

"Generator, why do we need one of those?"

"What do you mean...why do we need one of those?" said Fred mimicking the tone of Bill's voice. "How do you expect a laptop to work without power?"

"I don't know. I hadn't really thought about it."

"Why does that not surprise me?" said Fred sarcastically. Irritated, he snatched the laptop from him and marched into what was the front room. He pushed a light switch, and a grubby bulb hanging from the ceiling flickered into life. "I assume you prefer this to candles?" he said pointing at the bulb. "It's just as well one of us thinks ahead."

"Okay, no need to rub it in." Bill was embarrassed, and angry at himself for not thinking about it. "So where did you get the generator from?"

"I didn't. It was already here, but broken. I managed to get hold of a few parts and fixed it. It should last till we get the money."

Bill was impressed, but he would never admit it. "Well, I still don't think it's a suitable place to bring the boy." He frowned as he ran the back of his hand under his nose, attempting to stifle a sneeze.

Fred clenched his fists, rose to his full height and glared at him. "Quit moaning," he growled.

Bill saw the flash of anger in his cold dark eyes and backed away. He knew better than to push Fred.

Fred sneered at him; he found Bill's soft streak annoying. As far as he was concerned it smacked of weakness. But he knew he couldn't do the job alone. So, for the moment he would have to put up with him. "Like I told you before, we needed somewhere that was miles away from anywhere—this is it. And anyway, we won't be here for long. If you're so worried about the kids comfort, help me get the room sorted." He grabbed a blanket brought in from the car, and led the way upstairs to a small room at the rear of the house.

As with the rest of the building, the room was damp and unpleasant. Bill stared around, he noticed the door had a strong bolt on it, and the window seemed intact. A rusty iron bed and an old chair where the only furniture in the room.

Fred threw the thin blanket onto the bed and grinned, enjoying Bill's discomfort. "I think this accommodation will do nicely for our young guest, don't you?" He burst out laughing as he made his way back downstairs.

Bill said nothing as he followed him. He would just be glad when it was all over and they'd got what they came for.

Chapter 6

Jean drove home, her mind occupied with thoughts of Tom and the baby rat. She knew Tom was desperate to keep the rat and part of her hoped she would be unable to find the owner, but she had to try.

She had a few friends locally who kept pet rats. So once indoors she went to her desk and sorted through a few phone numbers. But those she rang informed her—their rats were present and correct. She really had no idea what to do next.

Over dinner she discussed the situation with her husband. "It's a real mystery Ken. The rat must be from around here somewhere. But I don't see how she could have travelled so far... she's too young."

"Well she obviously did. To have made it from our village to the Lewis's and in one piece is pretty amazing and in broad daylight too. I don't think even a wild rat would attempt that. If I were you I would let Tom keep her. I've watched him in church, he's lonely and it will do him good to have a pet."

"I agree with you, but I feel I should do my best to find the owner if I can. I will try for a couple more days, but if I have no luck, then I'll tell the Lewis's Tom can keep the rat, but if there're not keen, then I'm happy to take her."

Ken nodded in agreement.

For a few more days Jean continued her search, ringing round and making enquiries, but to no avail. It really was a mystery and Jean hated mysteries, but it looked like this one would remain unsolved.

Later in the week while Tom was at school, she returned to the Lewis's and had a coffee with Amy and Alice.

"No one appears to have lost a baby rat" she told them. "So as far as I'm concerned Tom can keep her, if it's okay with you Amy. How is she doing anyway?"

"Come and have a look." Amy led the way to the utility room. "She's a lot bigger now; I bet you'll hardly recognize her."

Mask heard them and came to the bars in the hope of a treat.

"My goodness!" exclaimed Jean. "You have grown young lady, good food and love works miracles." She turned to Amy. "So, how do you feel about Tom keeping her?" Amy's enthusiastic response surprised her.

"Not a problem Jean, we've become quite fond of her, including me. How's that for a miracle?" she laughed.

Jean was thrilled and glad her search for

Mask's owner had proved unsuccessful. She wanted Tom to keep Mask.

"You will need a cage for her," she advised. "If you like I could go to the pet shop with you and show you what you'll need to get."

Amy smiled with relief. Looking after a pet was a new experience for the family. "Thanks Jean that would be great, we could do with some help."

"No problem. Will Saturday be okay?"

"Yes, that would be good. Tom will be thrilled when I tell him he can keep the rat."

Jean was delighted. "That's settled then. I'll see you on Saturday."

❧❦

Tom could hardly contain himself when he heard the news. He ran to the utility room to tell Mask.

She was completely underwhelmed and just carried on eating. Her ears twitched as she listened to his voice...high pitched with excitement.

"We're going shopping for you in a couple of days," he told her. "And I shall buy you a really big cage." His eyes shone with enthusiasm.

"Don't you mean I will buy her a big cage?"

Taken by Surprise, Tom spun round; he could feel his face redden with embarrassment. "Yes, sorry dad".

"That's okay son, just make sure you don't let me down. You take good care of her."

"Oh I will, I promise."

Ben grinned and tousled Tom's hair. "I know you will and I'm glad you're happy."

❧❦

When Saturday came the house buzzed with excitement.

"I wish Mask could come as well," said Tom, grinning from ear to ear.

"Don't push your luck son," said Ben. He put his coat on and shouted up the stairs to Amy. "Jean's arrived, are you nearly ready?"

"Yes, I'm coming."

Brimming with excitement, Tom was already at the front door waiting.

"Jean's taking her car and we'll follow in ours." Ben explained as he helped Amy on with her coat.

"That's fine." Amy took his hand as they followed Tom to the car.

Jean smiled at Tom and waved. "See you at the store," she called.

He grinned and waved back.

The pet store was huge. As they went through the automatic doors it was hard to know where to begin.

"Follow me," said Jean. "I know this place like the back of my hand." She led them down the wide isles, ignoring the shelves packed to the rafters with numerous things for cats and dogs.

"Right, here we are." She halted in an area stocked with cages of various shapes and sizes, along with shelves overflowing with exciting

38

goodies for rabbits, hamsters, rats, and all things small and furry. Jean could see they were confused and quickly took the situation in hand.

In no time they found themselves at the till, complete with a cage and arms full of everything necessary for a pet rats health and happiness.

"You'll be fine now," she assured them, as they stood waiting to pay. "Do you mind if I nip off, I'll see you Sunday?"

"Fine, thanks for your help Jean, we really appreciate it," said Ben.

"Not a problem," she replied, and disappeared through the automatic doors and onto the car park.

෩෩

Mask seemed content in her new home. She disappeared into a large cardboard tunnel with a snack.

Ben stood beside Tom with his arm round his son's shoulders. "She looks happy."

Tom looked up at his father and grinned. "She is dad, thank you for letting me keep her."

Amy and Alice stood in the kitchen doorway watching them.

"It is nice to see them together like that," said Alice quietly. She looked at Amy noting her thoughtful expression.

Amy leaned against the door jam. "It is; but I do think it strange how the rat appeared as if from nowhere—still," she said with a slight smile. "It's good to see Tom so happy."

Alice wiped her hands on her apron and nodded in agreement.

Chapter 7

After the initial excitement of Mask's mysterious arrival, life soon returned to normal in the Lewis household. Ben was kept busy at the bank, while Amy occupied herself with the beauty parlour.

The whole family noticed the change in Tom. Gone the quiet withdrawn boy, now he was confident and cheerful, the house rang with his laughter. His school work noticeably improved and no one had to nag him to get on with his homework.

However, if his teachers had known that occasionally they had a secret attendee called Mask, they might not have been so pleased with him. His parents were also unaware she went to school with him, hidden in the large front pocket of his school bag. Fortunately for Tom, Mask was well behaved and happy in her secret hidey-hole, so no one found out.

As she grew the mask on her face became more distinct. She was extremely pretty and Tom adored her. They were inseparable and it wasn't long before she graduated from the utility room into Tom's bedroom, on the understanding he kept her cage clean.

Alice was not too happy at first and threatened dire consequences if the cage was anything but pristine.

"I don't know why I've let you talk me into this?" she grumbled, as between them they struggled to carry the cage complete with rat, upstairs to Tom's bedroom. They placed it on the floor by his bed. Tom watched with delight as Mask left her cardboard tunnel to look over her new surroundings.

"Thanks Alice, she likes it here." He threw his arms around her ample waist.

Alice grinned and ruffled his hair. "Maybe she does, but you remember what I said young man. If I smell anything remotely unpleasant coming from this room, she goes back downstairs, do you understand me?"

Tom looked up at her; he could see a slight twinkle in her eyes. He gave her a cheeky grin. "I will keep the cage clean, Alice, I promise."

"Well you make sure you do." She gazed fondly at his dark curls beneath her hand and smiled. From the first day she entered the Lewis household, young Tom was able to twist her around his little finger.

However, true to his promise, Tom kept the cage clean, giving his parents and Alice no cause for complaint.

Mask loved her new situation and enjoyed

roaming freely around his room. Wherever he was, she would never be far away. Tom quickly learned to watch where he put his feet, encase he trod on her, which he nearly did on numerous occasions. Only her loud squeak of protest diverted a possible disaster.

In no time, Mask learned her name and would come when he called, unless she happened to be doing something more interesting, like getting into mischief, or eating a favourite treat.

At other times she would sit on his desk, while he did his homework, nibbling the paper, chewing his pencils or running across the keys of his laptop.

But her favourite game was playing with him on the bed and trying to remove his socks. The room would resound with Tom's squeals of hysterical laughter.

Alice struggled to understand why suddenly most of his socks were full of holes.

Tom made every excuse he could think of, to keep them both out of trouble.

When he sneaked her into school, they would have their lunch in a secluded spot under a large oak tree, a short distance from the playground.

Tom would sit on the grass and eat his sandwiches, with Mask on his lap half hidden by his jacket. She loved the fresh dandelion leaves he picked for her.

Jean had told him how much rats enjoy them.

It was during one of these lunch breaks, that a couple of fellow pupils stumbled across him feeding Mask a bit of his cheese sandwich.

Mask, startled by their approach had vanished like a flash inside Tom's jacket, but not quickly enough.

Chess arrived first and gave Tom a knowing grin as he sprawled on the grass beside him. He was a big friendly lad around the same age as Tom. They were in the same class and knew each other well.

Chess's friend James a quiet and rather shy boy, trotted over and joined them. "What was that?" he asked, lowering his lanky frame to the ground beside Chess and staring suspiciously at Tom's jacket.

"It was a rat," said Chess.

"A rat! You're kidding me." James moved away from Tom his facial expression a picture of distaste.

Tom's brow creased in a troubled frown. He knew once his secret was out, he would no longer be able to bring Mask to school. And he didn't want to think about the trouble he would get into. He stared nervously from one boy to the other.

Chess noticed his worried expression and quickly reassured him. "It's okay, I like rats; in fact I have two of my own."

Surprised, Tom stared at him. "You didn't tell me you liked rats."

James scowled in distaste. "You didn't tell me either."

Chess grinned at James. "Well I knew you wouldn't be interested."

"So why didn't you tell me?" asked Tom.

"I would have been interested."

"Mum and dad said not to. They knew how much you wanted a pet. And anyway we only see each other at school or church; you've never been to my house."

"That's true, I suppose," said Tom.

Chess held his hands out. "Come on then, let me see it."

Tom retrieved Mask from under his jacket and handed her to him. "Don't lose her, she's quick." He needn't have worried, Chess handled her with confidence and Mask was quite relaxed.

James pursed his lips with distaste and watched nervously. He was not one for animals, especially rodents.

Chess handed Mask back to Tom. "She's cool and I like the black mask on her face."

"Thanks," said Tom concealing Mask inside his jacket. "You won't tell anyone I bring her to school, will you?"

Chess grinned at his anxious expression. "Don't worry; we'll keep your secret... won't we?" He poked James with his elbow.

"Yeh, I guess," mumbled James.

"Why don't you bring yours to school?" Tom asked.

"I don't think so, my boys would be everywhere. Miss Wells would freak out."

The boys burst into noisy laughter, as they shared a vision of their teacher standing on a chair, screaming and hanging onto her skirt.

Just then the school bell rang, Chess and James scrambled to their feet. "See you in class," they shouted as they ran to the playground.

Tom put Mask in the pocket of his school bag.

She was tired after all the excitement. She took a drink from the water bottle he carried for her then settled down for a nap.

Carefully, Tom put the bag across his shoulder and joined his class as they filed into school. He was relieved the pupils who had discovered his secret, were friends. He hoped he could trust them not to say anything.

Chapter 8

Bill and Fred scrambled to their feet cursing. They were hiding a few feet away from Tom, hidden from view behind a hedge.

"We'll have to try again tomorrow," grumbled Bill, puffing and blowing as he struggled to stand. His legs were stiff after crouching behind a bush for what seemed like ages. He grunted in frustration and ran a hand over his bald head...sticky with sweat.

Fred glared at him. "I told you we should have grabbed him yesterday, when he was alone."

"Look mate, we needed to make sure he was the right kid and thanks to those two boys, we know he is. So we'll just keep watch and grab him as soon as we can."

"Yeh, but what about that rat of his, I hate rodents!"

"I don't like them either, if it gives us a problem we'll kill it. But it could prove to be useful," said Bill.

"Oh yeh, and how do you make that out?" Fred scowled as he brushed bits of leaves and dirt off his trousers.

"Well, it could be a good way to convince the kid's folks we really do have their son."

Fred straightened up and thought about it for a moment, then nodded in agreement. "You could be right for once," he said sarcastically.

Bill made no comment as they forced their way through the thick shrubbery and back onto the road. Jumping into the battered green Ford, they drove away at great speed discussing the final plans for the kidnap of Tom.

An hour or so later they turned into the drive of the dilapidated old farm house. The sun was beginning to set. Long dark shadows crept over the ground, accentuating the bleakness of the place.

With a sigh of resignation, Bill eased his large bulk out of the car. Stony faced and grumbling under his breath, he followed Fred into the house. Instantly the unpleasant damp smell assailed his nostrils. "I still say this is no place to bring the kid, it stinks."

"Oh shut up, don't be so pathetic!" Fred snapped. "He's not coming for a holiday; we're kidnapping him for crying out loud. If you're that worried, go and check the room, see if you can make it more comfy and cosy for him."

Bill glared, he could see the mockery in Fred's eyes, but he knew better than to respond. In their short time together, he'd quickly sussed, Fred was not a man to cross, or argue with. Seething with annoyance, he made his way up the creaky stairs and along the dark passage to the small room prepared for Tom.

He glanced across at the bed. Even with the blanket thrown over it, it still looked grubby and uncomfortable. On the floor next to the bed was a faded threadbare rug. "I'd hate to think what's crawling around in that, he muttered."

He shivered and pulled his jacket closer, a distinct chill pervaded the room. It would be dark soon and the only source of light in the poky room apart from the window was a naked light bulb, hanging from the ceiling on a dangerous looking wire.

The atmosphere was dank and unpleasant. Bill grimaced; the musty smell irritated his nose. As he edged towards the door, he heard Fred yell from the kitchen.

"Check the lock on the door is secure and especially that window."

"Okay," he shouted back. He checked the door and went across to the window; he noticed work was needed on the catch. "I'll do it later, I need a cuppa." Hunched against the cold and moaning to himself, he went downstairs into the dingy kitchen, where Fred was making a brew.

"Is it okay up there?"

"Yeh, pretty much, but I'm still not happy about keeping the boy here."

"So you keep saying, you sound like a flaming cracked record, give it a rest."

Bill grabbed a mug and poured himself some tea. He took a couple of digestive biscuits and dunked them in the sweet brew. "Are you sure no one will hear that generator?" he asked.

"It makes a heck of a noise."

Fred rolled his eyes with irritation. "In case you haven't already noticed, we're miles away from anywhere." He picked up his mug of tea and led the way into what was the front room.

Like the rest of the house it was a mess. There were broken panes in the window and the room was full of dust and cobwebs. What remained of the carpet was thick with dirt and ancient stains. In one corner of the room stood an old dining table, on it was a laptop and a small printer. They grabbed a couple of chairs and sat down.

"Where's the camera?" asked Fred.

"Here, in my coat pocket." Bill handed it to him.

Fred grinned as he took it. "As soon as we get the kid we'll take the photos and that's where the rat will come in handy. Like you said his folks will recognize it and know we have their kid and mean business." His eyes shone with glee as he thought about it.

"I'm not sure using a laptop to write the ransom note is a good idea" said Bill nervously. "Why not cut letters out of a newspaper and do the note that way, it's safer and not so easy to trace."

Fred frowned impatiently at him. "Look, the laptop is fine. Once we get the money, we'll dump the kid where he can be found, smash the laptop and ditch it. No one will be able to trace us, so stop worrying. We're onto a winner and we'll soon be rich." He grinned, but there was a sinister glint in his eyes which made Bill uneasy.

He looked away unable to meet Fred's gaze. Secretly he wished he was anywhere but in this dank old house with Fred.

Chapter 9

Tom lifted Mask out of her cage and put her in the large front pocket of his school bag. "Right I'm taking you to school today, so you have to be good."

She watched him fill the pocket with soft tissue paper and busied herself tearing it up. In no time the large leather pocket resembled a cosy nest. Mask enjoyed her outings with Tom, each morning she would wait hopefully by the door of her cage.

"Don't forget now, you must be quiet," he whispered. "This is our secret." He gave her a small treat to nibble on, while he continued to get ready. It was fun taking her to school and she seemed to enjoy it, well, he assumed she did, as she never tried to run away.

When he was ready, he loosely closed the front of the pocket. She was already curled in a tight ball and half asleep. He smiled as he carefully put the bag over his shoulder and went downstairs to the kitchen.

Alice was busy wiping the table, she handed him his lunch box. "I won't be a minute, I just need to finish this, and then we can go."

His mother rushed into the kitchen. "I'm running a bit late. See you both later, have a good day. Make sure you come straight home from school Tom, as it get's dark early now."

"I will mum, see you later."

She gave him a kiss and flew out of the house like a whirlwind. All they could hear was the roar of the engine as she drove away.

"I do wish she wouldn't drive that fast," Alice muttered, as she picked up her car keys. "Okay Tom, let's get you to school."

Tom followed her to the car, he was relieved she didn't seem to check whether Mask was in her cage or not, or even notice the slight smell coming from his bag. Tom knew he was being dishonest, and he did feel guilty. But he loved taking Mask to school; it made him happy knowing she was with him.

The journey took no time at all. Tom said goodbye to Alice and made his way to class. At lunch time, he went to his usual place and sat on the grass. It was a mild autumn day, the sun was warm and the leaves rustled gently above his head. Chess said he would join him a bit later, but Tom was hungry and couldn't wait.

He took his sandwich box opened it and went to get Mask out of the pocket of his school bag...before he could, strong arms grabbed him from behind and covered his face with a cloth. A pungent and unpleasant smell invaded his senses. Unable to breathe he struggled and fought to push the hand away. He tried to scream but no sound escaped his throat. He felt as though he was falling...then nothing, just blackness.

"Get his school bag, quick," hissed Fred. "Hurry up."

"But that's where he keeps the rat." Bill stared at the bag with distaste.

"Pick it up you coward," snapped Fred impatiently. He scooped Tom into his arms, ran through the trees and dropped him onto the rear seat of the car.

Bill followed holding the bag at arm's length; his hands trembled slightly with apprehension. His eyes were glued to the pockets, any sign of movement and he was ready to drop it. Grateful to reach the car, he plonked it on the seat beside Tom's unconscious body. "Just because you hate rodents more than me, I have to carry the bag." He complained. "That rat had better not get loose in the car."

Fred scowled at him. "Forget the blasted rat, hurry up and get in. We don't want to be seen and the chloroform will wear off in an hour or so." Fred slammed his foot on the accelerator and drove like mad through endless country lanes, eventually arriving at the old farm house. By this time Tom was beginning to stir. They skidded to a halt and Fred dragged him from the car. He glanced impatiently at Bill. "Bring the bag, hurry up."

Fred carried Tom upstairs. "I'll put him in the chair; you tie him up for the moment."

"Why? The rooms secure."

"Just do it," snapped Fred. He chucked a length of course rope at him. "I need to get my thoughts together." He paced the room staring at Tom's unconscious form.

Bill shrugged...dumped the bag onto the floor and quickly moved away wiping his hands disdainfully on his jacket. "Well, if the rat escapes here, it should feel at home." He tied Tom's hands and feet to the chair. A twinge of guilt tugged at him as he looked at the small helpless boy, but he shrugged it off, there was nothing he could do. They'd grabbed him, so now they had to go through with it. He turned away, locked the door and followed Fred downstairs into the front room. "Should I have put the light on for him? It'll be dark soon"

"No, leave him be, he's here for one reason and one reason only. He's our meal ticket and this ain't a flippin hotel. And anyway if his dad plays ball he'll be out of here in a day or two. He's still groggy, so he'll be okay for a while and it gives us a chance to finish the letter, then we'll take the photo before he comes round. The sooner we make contact with his father, the sooner we get the money and get away from here."

Bill nodded in agreement. At least it looked like their plan was coming together. Soon he hoped he would be rich beyond his wildest dreams. He knew if he kept his mind on the financial rewards, he wouldn't feel so guilty about the boy.

Chapter 10

It was just after two o'clock; Alice was finishing her lunch when the phone rang. It was Tom's teacher Miss Wells and she sounded concerned.

"I just thought I should let Mrs Lewis know that Tom hasn't returned to class. I wondered if he had an appointment this afternoon and she forgot to tell us."

Alice frowned, her knuckles whitened as she clutched her apron. "As far as I know, he doesn't. I can't imagine where he could be... this is rather worrying. Maybe I should ring his father."

"Yes, I think you should, this is not like Tom, please keep me informed."

"We will." Alice's hand shook as she rang Ben. He tried to appear calm, but Alice could tell by his voice he was worried.

"Okay Alice I'm coming home, but don't ring Amy just yet, there may be nothing wrong. Do you know if Tom has his phone with him?"

"I don't know, I didn't see it, but he knows he should always keep it with him, so I'm sure he has, he's a sensible boy."

"Well stay by the phone in case he rings, I'll be home shortly."

Restless with worry, Alice paced the floor, desperately trying not to think the worst. Frightening scenarios rolled around in her head. Hearing Ben's key in the door, she rushed to meet him.

"Is there any news?" He asked.

"No nothing." She could see the concern in his eyes. Her heart fluttered with apprehension as she followed him into the office. "Should we ring Mrs Lewis now?" Her voice trembled with anxiety.

Ben nodded the phone was already in his hand. "Amy its Ben—Alice rang me at the office; Tom's teacher has been in touch. It seems he's not returned to class and as yet no one knows where he is." He made no attempt now to hide his concern.

On the other end of the phone—Amy's heart leapt into her mouth. "Oh Ben this is awful where could he be? You sound worried."

"I am sweetheart. I think you should come home."

"I'm on my way." Amy replaced the receiver. Her heart pounded—she felt sick—shaky. Leaving hurried instructions for her staff, she drove home as fast as she could.

Ben heard the car screech to a halt and hurried to the front door.

Amy rushed into his arms. "What do you

think has happened to him Ben, where is he? This is just not like him."

"I don't know where he is, but we must try not to panic. We need to stay calm and think."

She looked into his eyes; he knew what she was thinking. Her lips trembled as she voiced their thoughts. "Oh God Ben, do you think someone has taken him?" she burst into tears.

He had no answers; all he could do was hold her close. "We won't go down that road Amy unless we have too. I need to make some phone calls...he could be at a friend's house, or any where."

"But his friends are still at school," replied Amy wiping tears from her eyes.

"I know, but I have to do something." His hand shook slightly as he picked up the phone and dialled the headmaster's number. He needed to keep busy or go mad.

Amy and Alice rang some of the other parents.

Ben's conversation with Forsyth the headmaster was not encouraging. His heart sank as he listened.

Forsyth explained that a lad called Chess had arranged to meet Tom in the lunch break. However, when Chess arrived Tom was nowhere to be seen, just sandwiches scattered over the ground. "He came to tell me and I followed him to the spot—all we found was Tom's empty lunch box. It looked like he'd left in a hurry. I'm sorry Mr Lewis, I don't want to worry you, but I am concerned. I really think you should inform the police."

Ben agreed with him, it was now four thirty and beginning to get dark, and still no sign of Tom. So with his heart in his mouth, Ben rang the local police station.

They seemed to arrive in seconds. The two men oozed confidence as they walked into the house.

"I'm detective inspector Mullins," said the larger man, extending his hand to Ben. "And this is Sergeant Buoyed." He nodded at the tall man standing beside him.

Ben shook his outstretched hand; the grip was firm and reassuring.

"Right sir, we all need to stay calm and not jump to any wrong conclusions." He gazed at their panic stricken faces and knew right away his confident words had fallen on deaf ears. Undaunted, he continued, he could not allow them to go into panic mode.

"I've dispatched a couple of officers to the school; they'll have a good look round and ask a few questions. It's too soon to start worrying; your son could have gone for a walk...or anything. We all know what boys can be like, don't we? I have two of my own." He attempted a reassuring smile. "How was he getting on at school?" He saw Amy's face flush pink with annoyance and wished he didn't have to ask such questions.

Amy knew what he was hinting at, but managed to suppress her irritation. In as calm a voice as possible, she told him. "Tom enjoys school and is doing well. If you talk to his teachers you'll find this to be true. I can't believe he wouldn't return to class. He's a responsible boy; he wouldn't just go off. I know he wouldn't." Her voice rose as she fought to control her emotions.

Alice put an arm round her; she loved Tom too, like he was her own son. She feared the thoughts crashing around in her head, but did her best to comfort Amy.

Mullin's tried to hide his concern from them. The Lewis's were a wealthy family, with a high profile in the area—the possibility of kidnap had to be faced. Mullin's didn't want to voice his thoughts, but he knew he might well have to, especially when one of the officers at the school rang him with worrying news.

The officer informed him that Tom's lunch box was found on the ground and it looked as though there had been some sort of struggle.

Mullins sighed. "Keep searching," he told the officer. He didn't want to assume the worst, until he was forced to.

The Lewis's stared at him, aware something was wrong.

Amy began to cry and almost collapsed onto the couch.

Ben and Alice sat beside her.

Mullins faced them, his expression grim. As gently as he could, he tried to explain that kidnap was becoming a distinct possibility. "If that's the case," he said. "Then we should hear from the kidnappers within the next twenty four hours. If someone has taken your son, they'll be in touch soon—guaranteed."

"Oh God—Ben—what are we going to do?"

Amy clutched his hand.

Ben had no answers; all he could do was hold her close. "We are going to keep calm and trust God," he replied, hoping she couldn't hear his heart pounding.

At that moment sergeant Buoyed came into the room, he looked worried. He motioned to Mullins; the D.I followed him into the hall.

"I've just received a call sir, from one of the constables at the school. He and the other officer had a good look round the area where Tom had his lunch. They found a gap in the hedge which opened onto a quiet road. There were a lot of fresh footprints; it could be the way the boy was taken out of the school grounds unseen.

A farmer working in the field opposite, told them he noticed an old green car; he thinks it was a Ford...parked just down the road. He mentioned it, as the car was there at the same time for three days running, which he thought was rather strange."

Mullins ran a hand through his greying hair; a worried frown creased his brow. "Was it by any chance the same time Tom used to have his lunch?"

Sergeant Buoyed nodded.

"So, it looks like he was being watched. I best go and tell his parent's, what a mess and on my patch too!" He walked slowly into the sitting room; he hated this part of his job, especially when it involved children.

The Lewis's and Alice, were still sitting where he'd left them, they watched him approach.

He could feel their eyes boring into him, trying to gauge his expression. They knew what he was going to say before he opened his mouth.

"Someone's taken him, haven't they?" cried Alice, tears trickled down her face.

Ben patted her hand. There was nothing he could say.

She sobbed as he attempted to comfort her.

Amy said nothing, she sat beside him pale and stunned.

Mullins sat opposite and as gently as he could...told them what he'd just heard.

In the ensuing silence; you could have heard a pin drop. It was as though a strange calm came over them.

"At least now we know what we're up against," said Ben, there was a gritty edge to his voice. He rose from the couch, his handsome face set like stone. "Whatever it takes—whatever they want—we do it."

Mullins tried to explain the different ways the kidnappers might get in touch. "They could use the phone, so just in case I'll call the station and get my people here, we need to tap into the kidnapper's call when it comes. If they get in touch by letter it could be more difficult. Either way nothing much will happen until tomorrow. I know it's hard, but please, try and keep calm. I'll leave sergeant Buoyed here with you tonight; he will be in constant touch with me. I need to get to the station and sort things out, but I'll return first thing tomorrow."

Ben walked with him to the front door.

"Tell me Mr Lewis, what is Tom's temperament like. Would you say he's a strong boy?"

"Yes, he is, he may be only nine but he's an independent and confident boy. And he has a strong faith."

Relieved, Mullins shook Ben's hand. "That's good to hear sir and believe me we will get him home, safe and unharmed."

Ben thanked him and closed the door. For a brief moment he rested against it, feeling the solid strength of the wood against his back and wishing that same strength could be his. This was the nightmare he'd always dreaded...hoped and prayed would never happen. *Could he believe the Inspectors promise that they would find Tom and get him home safely*?

His stomach knotted, terrifying thoughts crashed around in his head, his heart was beating so fast, it hurt. He could feel the colour drain from his face. *I must pull myself together; I need to be strong, for Amy's sake, and Alice.* He forced himself away from the door, straightened and took a few deep breaths. He gazed heavenwards and quietly prayed. He knew this was going to be the longest night of their lives.

Chapter 11

Tom raised his head and let out a moan, his neck ached. He moved his head from side to side in an effort to ease the stiffness, he felt groggy and a bit sick. He went to move his arms and to his horror realized he was tied to a chair. *What happened, where am I?* For a moment he sat still trying to clear his head and listening to the creaks and groans of the old building.

Bit by bit, he remembered. Someone had grabbed hold of him and covered his face with something horrid and smelly. He shuddered at the memory. Desperate and afraid he fought against the ropes, but they were too tight.

Like an arrow, a sudden thought shot into his head—*my school bag! Where is it—where's Mask?* Frantic, he looked around trying to see as best he could in the dim light. Thoughts of Mask lost and afraid almost paralyzed him. He fought against the stinging tears. Struggling to remain calm, his eyes searched every inch of the room. To his relief, he saw the bag lying on the floor in the far corner. Tom stared at it, willing Mask to be safe in the pocket, quietly he prayed.

"Please, let Mask be in the bag." As he prayed an idea began to take shape in his mind and a fragile hope slowly replaced his fear and despair. With his eyes glued to the bag, he called her name as quietly as he could. "Oh God," he whispered. "Let her be there, I need her to come to me." Softly he called again. "Mask, come here girl. Mask...please." To Tom's relief the bag moved and a little face appeared from the pocket. Desperate, he continued to call her.

Slowly...tentatively Mask climbed out of the school bag and scuttled across to him.

"Great, come on Mask, here," he moved his feet about to encourage her.

She clambered up his trousers and went to her favourite place on his shoulder. Traumatized and trembling, she snuggled against his neck.

"Good girl." Tom gently rubbed his cheek against her. "Mask, I need you to gnaw through these ropes," he whispered. "Come on, please, you can do it, pretend it's my socks." Tom knew she didn't understand what he was saying. It would be a miracle if she did, but he had to try. He was brought up to believe in miracles.

He had no idea how long they'd been there, but now it was dark and he guessed some one would come soon. Frantically, he wiggled his fingers around to try and attract her. He had to move fast, but he knew he must stay calm. His fear would transmit to her and in this strange place she might panic and run away. The thought of losing her was unbearable.

As he sat there a thought came to him, she might do it if she thought it was a game. In as bright a tone as he could muster, he whispered. "Where's those sock's Mask? You hate socks."

Recognising the tone of his voice, she relaxed and began washing herself.

"Oh, no Mask." Tom tried not to panic. "There's no time for washing, you can do that later. We must get away from here." He nudged her with his chin and wiggled his fingers as vigorously as he could. The ropes where tight and burned his wrists. "Oh God please, I need her to go to the rope."

As the words left his mouth— she yawned—stretched and moved away from his face. She balanced precariously on the edge of his shoulder sniffing the air. Then slowly she made her way down his arm towards his hands.

Tom dare not move or make a sound. He held his breath...prayed she wouldn't jump to the floor and go exploring. *Please Mask, go for the ropes.*

Slowly, she continued down his arm until she came to his bound wrists.

Frantically, Tom wiggled his fingers to attract her. It worked; she sniffed the ropes and started to pull at them, just as she would have done with his socks. To his relief she started to chew the rope, he could hardly believe it. Her sharp nails bit into his skin, but Tom hardly felt the pain he was so elated.

Occasionally she would stop and sniff the air. Tom hardly dare breathe... desperate for her to keep going. He was terrified she would get distracted or worse jump to the ground. He moved his fingers constantly to encourage her. He could hear her teeth tearing through the rope as though it was butter. It seemed to take forever, but, in a few seconds his hands were free. He was so glad she hated socks, plasters, bandages, or anything else she thought didn't belong on him.

Overjoyed, Tom scooped her up in his hands and hugged her. "You can put as many holes in my socks as you like from now on," he whispered. Gently, he placed her on his shoulder, while he untied the rope around his ankles. He stood and stretched, his whole body felt stiff and sore, but the joy of freedom erased the discomfort from his mind.

He tiptoed across the creaky floor, retrieved his bag and carefully put Mask in the front pocket. In his trouser pocket he had a small bar of chocolate. He bit off a tiny piece and gave it to her, she loved chocolate. Tom would have given her the whole bar he was so grateful, but it wasn't good for her.

He left her eating and crept to the window. He knew this could be his only means of escape. As he inspected it, he could hardly believe his luck. The window had a broken catch. Tom peered through the dirty glass, but it was too dark to see anything. He guessed he was in an upstairs room and hoped it was no higher than the first floor. He struggled against the desire to panic. He hated heights and prayed he would reach the ground safely.

Breathing hard and with trembling hands he eased the window up. It was stiff and made a little noise, but he managed to move it and pushed it halfway before it stuck. *That's okay, I'm small. I can squeeze through there.*

He tiptoed back across the room and picked up his bag, checking Mask was safe in the pocket. "I'm going to climb out of the window, so stay in there," he whispered. He fastened the pocket, and put the strap of the bag over his head. With the bag secure across his body, he made his way as quietly as possible to the window. The floorboards creaked at every step. He held his breath afraid he would be heard.

Reaching the window he put his head through the gap and stared into the darkness, waiting until his eyes adjusted. He sighed with relief when he noticed a drainpipe attached to the wall and realized he was only on the first floor. Nevertheless, he trembled with fear at the thought of climbing down the drainpipe. *I hope it can hold me. It looks old and rickety.* He shivered and pulled his jacket closer.

For a brief second he looked back into the room and listened...all was quiet. Desperate to get away, Tom ducked under the window and bravely eased onto the narrow ledge. He sat there trembling and staring into the darkness. *Oh God I hope I can do this.* Frozen with fear, he stared at the rusty drainpipe, praying his weight wouldn't pull it away from the wall and send him crashing to the ground.

Chapter 12

Tom eased along the window ledge until he was close enough to grab the drainpipe. He seized it firmly with both hands, then, with his heart in his mouth, he let himself swing off the ledge into thin air. He grimaced with pain as his upper body banged into the pipe; he hung there breathless...afraid to move. He was terrified the rusty pipe would pull away from the wall, plunging him to the ground. Or even worse, his captors might have heard the noise and be coming to investigate.

Tom's arms burned as he struggled to hang on. He looked down but it was too dark to see. He knew he couldn't hold on for much longer, he had to move. Tentatively, he gripped the pipe with his feet, which eased the pressure slightly on his arms. His breath came in frightened gasps as he slowly began to descend.

The rust on the drainpipe was sharp as splinters and bit into his hands, but he gritted his teeth and kept going. Each movement caused the fragile pipe to creak a loud protest. The nails holding it to the wall threatened to pull away and leave him swinging in mid-air—or worse.

His descent was slow and painful; he prayed his captors wouldn't hear him as he made his escape. Inch by inch he lowered himself down, it seemed to take forever. Then, all of a sudden his foot touched something wet... it turned out to be a water barrel. Thankfully he managed to avoid a ducking and was soon safely on the ground. He stood for a second to get his bearings. Rusty splinters stuck to his hands, he winced as he carefully wiped them against his jacket.

Tom's eyes quickly adjusted to the dark, but he had no idea were he was. He needed to find a road and get as far away as possible. Quietly he crept around the side of the house until he reached the front. He noticed a light on in one of the downstairs rooms and quickly pulled back into the shadows. Ahead of him, he could see a long driveway disappearing into darkness. *There must be a road at the end of it. I'm going to have to move fast.*

He secured the school bag under his arm. "I have to run Mask and I don't want you to fall out of the pocket." He took a deep breath, and sprinted as fast as he could down the drive, hardly daring to believe he'd managed to escape. But he knew they would come after him.

At the end of the drive he came to a crossroads. He stood for a moment to catch his breath. He chewed his lip as he stared nervously up and down the dark country lane. Frightened and confused he tried to remain calm, but his pounding heart betrayed his fear. *Which way should I go, left or right?* As he stood there he felt a strange urge to go left.

For a brief moment he turned and gazed longingly at the farm house. It seemed to be the only source of light for miles around and looked so welcoming— whereas the road facing him was as black as pitch.

He gazed anxiously into the darkness. "Oh mask, if I don't hurry they'll catch us, but it's so dark and I don't know where to go." With his heart in his mouth Tom stepped onto the road. Unable to see clearly he couldn't risk running, so he walked as fast as he could keeping to what he hoped was the middle of the road.

Cold and afraid, he shivered. *Surely there's a house or a farm somewhere around here*, but there was nothing, just all-embracing blackness. It clung to him like a heavy coat. He rubbed his tired eyes; they felt gritty and burned from straining to see.

The different sounds of the night freaked him out, especially when an owl hooted eerily above his head. Trees like tall dark monsters loomed over him, reaching out with long sinewy arms.

As he followed the narrow road, gradually his eyes adjusted to the darkness. He was frightened, but so grateful Mask was with him. "I'm going to get off this road," he told her. "If I can find somewhere to hide, maybe they won't find us." Tom knew while he was on the road, his kidnappers had every chance of catching him.

But if he could lie low somewhere, at least till morning, maybe he would have some idea where he was and be able to make good his escape.

Now that his eyes were accustomed to the darkness, he increased his pace. As he walked along, to his right he saw a break in the trees. Quickly he walked over to take a look; it was the entrance to a field, a large five bar gate blocked access. Tom went to open it, but found it padlocked. "No problem," he muttered to himself.

Wasting no time, he secured his school bag and clambered over the gate. Strangely it didn't seem so dark in the field. Scattered around were a number of small hay stacks. Tom hurried to the furthest stack and flopped down behind it. He was well hidden from the road.

He put his school bag on the ground and checked Mask, she seemed fine. There was still a little water in her bottle which she gratefully accepted. As he watched her drink, hot salty tears trickled down his face; he wiped them away with the back of his hand. The shock of being kidnapped suddenly hit him. He was hungry, thirsty and tired—fear hounded him. He wanted his mother and father.

Mask, however, was wide awake and frisky, so for awhile Tom played with her. It took his mind off his troubles and made him smile. But he was exhausted, his eyes ached with tiredness. He struggled to stay awake, knowing that if he fell asleep, Mask might wander off and he would lose her. But he desperately needed to rest. So he decided to put her in the main part of his school bag, where she would have more room to move around.

"Now you stay there Mask, chew my books if you want, but please don't run away." She took him at his word and began to investigate his pencil case and chew his exercise books. Tom grinned as he buckled the flap. He knew she could escape, but he hoped the contents of his bag would amuse her long enough for him to have a rest.

With his arm over the bag, he lay back in the hay and closed his eyes. In less than a minute he was asleep, dreaming of home and having dinner with his parents and Alice.

Chapter 13

Downstairs in the old farm house, Bill and Fred struggled to put a ransom demand together. Neither of them was computer literate, so it took longer than expected. They were both becoming increasingly irritable and frustrated, especially Fred, who was bad tempered at the best of times.

Bill found a glass in the kitchen and poured himself a large whisky, he needed to calm down. "Do you want one?"

"Yeh," said Fred snatching the glass from him.

Bill couldn't find another glass, so he poured the whisky into a chipped mug. He downed the amber liquid in one thirsty gulp. The whisky coursed warmly through his veins, he sighed and leaned back in his chair. His eyes creased with amusement as he watched Fred grapple with the laptop...cursing and muttering to himself.

As Bill sat there enjoying his drink, he heard a strange noise and jumped to his feet. The sound seemed to come from outside. "Did you hear that?"

"Hear what?" grunted Fred.

"I heard a thump and a grating sound, should I go check on the kid?" he headed for the door.

"No, leave him, he's tied up, so he ain't going anywhere and I need to get this finished. This house is full of strange noises ignore it."

Happy to oblige, Bill poured himself another whisky and sat down.

Eventually between them they managed to put a ransom note together.

"Right, is that it?" Bill put his empty mug on the table and stood up. "Let's print it and go and take the photo."

Fred scowled as he turned on the printer. "You're always in such a flaming hurry."

Bill said nothing, but his eyes darkened with annoyance. Fred made him nervous and he regretted joining him. *Why did I go to the pub that day? And why did he have to come and sit at my table? Soon as I saw him, I didn't like him, so why didn't I just walk out? Now it's too late.* He frowned at the memory. He'd only gone to the pub for a few pints and was sitting at a table in the corner, when Fred joined him.

Bill was short of cash and he couldn't help showing interest, when Fred boasted in a hushed voice about his plan to burgle the home of a rich banker. Bill, having downed a few pints of beer, found himself going along with Fred's plan. Now he was seriously thinking he might have made a big mistake.

Initially, the plan had been to burgle the banker's house, but when they heard he had a son, they decided it would be easier and more profitable just to kidnap the kid. But now concern weighed heavy on Bill...the longer he spent in Fred's company, the more he realised what a nasty piece of work he was. If things went wrong, Bill worried that Fred might harm the boy.

The sound of the printer switching off brought him back to reality. He grabbed the camera and followed Fred upstairs.

"Where's the key to the door?" asked Fred.

Bill pulled it out of his pocket. "I've got it." He unlocked the door and flipped the light switch.

They stood in the doorway hardly able to believe what they were seeing. The room was empty—the kid had vanished. All that remained was the rope coiled on the floor like a slumbering serpent.

Fred picked it up and stared in disbelief. "You couldn't have tied him securely." His face reddened with fury. He dropped the rope and stormed across to the half open window. "You fool! I told you to fix this." He swung round— fists clenched—eyes blazing. He moved towards Bill, his eyes dark and menacing.

Bill backed away with his hands in the air. "Look mate, let's keep calm. If we waste time fighting he'll be miles away, let's get the car and go after him. He can't have gone far, it's dark; we'll find him, easy."

Fred scowled and shoved him aside. He

raced down the stairs, his face crimson with anger.

Bill followed more slowly, fear clawed at him. There was no way he wanted to tangle with Fred.

They jumped in the car and raced towards the main road. The tyres spun in their search for purchase on the muddy drive. They came to the road and screeched to a halt.

Fred punched the steering wheel. "Which way has he gone?" He stared left and right, growling with frustration.

"Try left," Bill suggested. "If we don't find him we can come back this way."

"You better be right," said Fred pulling onto the road.

"Well, you should have listened to me when I said I heard a noise. I knew something was wrong." Bill was determined not to take all the blame, even though he knew the kids escape was down to him.

Fred glared at him. "Don't say another word," he warned ominously. "I hope for your sake we find him."

They drove in a tense silence, the car headlights blazing as they followed the narrow twisting lane. But their search proved fruitless.

Enraged, Fred banged his fist on the steering wheel. "There's no sign of him, he can't have got this far, we should have seen him by now."

"Well maybe he left the road and found somewhere to hide." Bill suggested. "He seems like a bright kid."

Fred ignored him and pulled into a lay-by. He spun the car round and accelerated away like a madman.

"Where are you going?" Bill nervously clutched his seat belt.

"We passed a gate into a field somewhere back here, I'm gonna have a look just in case."

They found the gate and he pulled the car off the road.

"Why are you bothering to look in a field?" Bill asked, as he squeezed out of the small car.

"Call it a hunch, but I want to have a quick look. He's just a kid, he'll be frightened and tired...a hay field's a good place to hide and rest." He went to the boot of the car, grabbed a torch and a cane stick. "Come on, hurry up." He strode to the gate and jumped it like a long legged horse.

Bill huffed and puffed as he followed him. "Hang on," he shouted.

Fred turned and shone the torch on him. "Get a move on, we don't have all night." He marched into the field grumbling and muttering to himself.

Bill clambered over the gate; all he could see in the thick darkness was the bobbing light of the torch. He caught up with Fred and followed him from hay stack—to hay stack.

Seething with rage, Fred poked his cane into each hay-stack, tossing hay everywhere—but no sign of the boy. "He has to be here somewhere," he growled. Using the cane like a sword, he thrust it deep into another small stack.

They were getting close to where Tom was

hiding—all of a sudden the heavens opened and it started to pour with rain.

"Blast! That's all we need." Fred spun round and headed back towards the gate.

"We haven't finished looking," Bill shouted after him.

"Forget it, if he's in this field he'll lay low till morning which is only a couple of hours away. I'm gonna drive round the lanes till dawn just in case he's trying to make a run for it."

They climbed over the gate and got into the car.

"Why don't we just stay here until it stops raining?"

Fred ignored him and started the engine, he had to keep busy or go mad with rage. He was sure if the kid was hiding among the hay stacks, he wouldn't move while it was dark. So it did no harm to check the lanes just in case, he could be wandering around lost. They had to get him back, he was their meal ticket.

He glared at Bill. "If we don't find him—" His threat petered out as he accelerated away from the field. He could hardly contain himself he was so angry.

Bill secured his seat belt and stared straight ahead. He was nervous, beads of perspiration glistened on his forehead. He knew he should have fixed the window catch. He sneaked a quick look at Fred. *I just hope we find the kid soon, before he blows a gasket*. His hand shook as he wiped sticky beads of sweat off his brow and stared out of the window. The car headlights picked out, trees, bushes... a fox crouched at the side of the road, but no sign of the boy.

Chapter 14

Tom woke with a start! He heard voices. Half asleep, he peered over the top of the haystack and saw the light flashing to and fro. Instantly, he knew it was the kidnappers! A wave of fear like icy fingers crawled up his spine. He grabbed his bag and pushed deeper into the hay. He knew if he moved they would see him, all he could do was keep his head down and pray for help. He held his breath and tried not to panic as they drew closer to his hiding place, *oh God, please help me*!

A sudden clap of thunder broke the silence...followed by a heavy downpour of rain. Tom could hear the men grumbling and then silence.

He waited for a while not sure if it was safe, but decided to take a risk. Cautiously, he poked his head out of the hay. In the distance he could just make out the bobbing light of a torch as the men made their way towards to the gate.

He opened his school bag and lifted Mask

out. "It's raining, so they've gone," he whispered. "But we can't stay here. I'm sure they'll come back."

Mask wriggled out of his hands and jumped into the wet hay glad to stretch her legs.

Tom quickly caught hold of the base of her tail. "Sorry Mask, I know you want to run around but you can't, you'll get lost—or worse." He put her onto his shoulder, where she settled and began to groom.

It was still dark, but Tom knew they had to make a move. He was convinced the men would return. He huddled in the wet hay, shivering with cold and fear. Hunger gnawed at his stomach. Tears fell, he couldn't stop them; desperation and loneliness overwhelmed him. Shuddering with emotion, he pulled a grubby hankie from his trouser pocket and blew his nose.

Mask sniffed his ear as if to comfort him, she could sense his distress.

Tom lifted her off his shoulder. "Ooh, Mask, you're all wet and cold. I don't think I'll put you in my school bag, you can go in my jacket pocket where you'll be warm and safe." He found her water bottle, but she refused it. "I don't suppose you're hungry either, are you? It looks like you've been eating my books." He grinned as he looked at what was left of his school work. "Well, I hope they tasted good."

He rose to his feet and put the bag over his shoulder; it definitely looked the worse for wear and smelled decidedly ratty.

The rain had stopped. Tom ran a hand

through his wet hair...his clothes felt damp and clammy. He looked at his wrist watch and frowned. It was too dark to see the time. He gazed into the sky, soft fingers of light heralded the dawn. He had a feeling; soon, the men would return to the field and continue searching for him. So, it was now or never—he must go—or be caught.

He put his hand inside his jacket and stroked Mask, she gently nibbled his finger. "I'm not going back to the gate," he told her. "I'll go across this field and see what's on the other side. Maybe we'll find a house and get help."

He trekked across the field; the ground under foot was soggy and hard going. His shoes were soon heavily caked with mud. He was glad his mother and Alice couldn't see him in this state, but he knew if he thought about them it would upset him, so he pulled himself together. He was convinced his father would be moving heaven and earth to find him. The thought comforted him and gave him the strength to keep going.

In the distance he could see a dark mass, which seemed to cover a vast area. He trudged on and eventually encountered another five bar gate. Beyond the gate was a dark forest which to young Tom appeared to go on for ever. He scrambled over the gate and found himself on a narrow country lane.

Desperate for help he looked around, searching for any pin-pricks of light, but there was nothing...not a house in sight. He knew if he stayed on the lane the kidnappers would find him.

To his right he noticed a muddy path. It disappeared into the dense forest of trees. The thought of walking alone in the forest scared him, but he had no other choice. He knew he must keep away from the roads and put as much distance as possible between himself and his pursuers.

He said a quick prayer and bravely followed the path. In an instant the forest surrounded him and he vanished, swallowed by a cloak of darkness.

Chapter 15

Bill and Fred having spent a fruitless few hours driving around the lanes, returned to the field. If Tom was there, they hoped to catch him before it got light. They didn't want to give him a chance to make a run for it. They strode across the field towards the remaining hay stacks.

Bill struggled to keep up with Fred, puffing and blowing in an effort to catch his breath.

It was getting light and the early risers in the bird world were already welcoming what promised to be a sunny autumn day.

As they approached the last hay stack, the one Tom had been hiding in; they could hardly contain their excitement. Hay was strewn over the ground and there was a small hole in the main stack where Tom had crawled out. They grabbed handfuls of the hay, throwing it everywhere in a desperate effort to get at him, unaware he'd already gone. When the truth eventually dawned, they stood there fuming.

Covered with bits of straw, they resembled irate scarecrows.

Fred's eyes blazed with anger, his cheeks burned red. He was so enraged he could hardly speak. "This is down to you," he growled at Bill.

"Look mate, I'm sorry, what can I say?"

Fred glared and grabbed him by the front of his shirt. He stuck a clenched fist in his face. "If he gets away, you'll be sorry." He pushed Bill aside and strode back across the field to the gate. As he walked he brushed bits of hay off his clothes, all the while cursing and growling to himself.

Bill followed at a distance, his face creased in a worried frown. *That was a close call.* Agitated, he wiped his sweaty hands on his jacket. Fred's body language did little to ease his anxiety. Bill knew Tom's escape was down to him and the little he knew about Fred was enough to convince him...if they didn't find the kid soon, he could be in some danger.

"Get a move on," Fred yelled, as he leapt with ease over the gate.

Bill walked as fast as he could, but his weight made him blow...he struggled to get his breath. He scrambled over the gate and forced his ample frame into the car. "Where are we going now?" He asked between painful gasps.

"Back to the house where do you think? I'm sending the ransom note to the kid's parents."

Confused, Bill stared at him. "You're kidding me! We don't have the boy, so how can we send a ransom note?"

Fred rolled his eyes and sneered in frustration. He floored the accelerator, the old car screeched away from the gate, leaving behind a shower of mud.

"Were you born stupid?" he growled. "Didn't you see the mess at that last haystack?"

"Yeh, I did, but so what?"

"Well, if you'd looked closely you would have seen small footprints. It looks like the kid did a runner just before we arrived and he's headed across the field towards the forest?"

"Are you sure?" A flicker of concern crossed Bill's face. "A kid his age will get well lost if that's the way he's going."

Fred grinned. "Exactly, they will have paid us the ransom by the time he's found. That forest goes for miles and if he ever gets out, he'll find it's just open fields. Our farm is the only property for miles round here." A cruel smile creased his hard face. "It's not over yet."

Bill sat thinking, it seemed too easy...a thought crossed his mind.

"But what about the photographs, surely we need to prove we have him? I mean they won't just pay up."

Fred pulled up outside the farm house and switched off the engine. "We'll cross that bridge when we come to it," he said easing his lanky frame out of the car. He strode into the house and led the way into the front room. "Just leave it to me I'll handle it. Once they have the letter and I phone them with instructions for the drop, they'll be desperate to give us the money."

Still not totally convinced, Bill bravely

asked. "But what if the police are already involved? They won't let them part with any money, they'll want proof. I don't like it"

Furious, Fred swung round with clenched fists, his eyes flashed. "I don't care what you like. If you'd fixed the window catch like I told you, the kid would still be safely locked in the room. We lost him because of you!" He continued to rant as he stuffed the letter into an envelope, addressed it and made for the door.

"Where are you going?" asked Bill nervously.

"To the post office, where do you think?" He stormed out of the house, climbed into the car and roared away.

Bill knew he would be gone some time, so he went to the kitchen and put the kettle on, he needed a brew. He was worried; things were not turning out as he'd hoped. He frowned as he dropped a tea bag in his mug. *This could get nasty, but I dare not back out now. I'll have to see it through to the end and just hope I get something out of it, but more importantly—not get caught.*

He was concerned for the boy; he meant him no real harm. The kid was just a means to an end. But he would never trust Fred. In one way he was glad the kid had managed to escape, at least he was out of Fred's clutches. *The only trouble is, now he could be in even greater danger.* Bill sighed. "What a mess," he muttered.

He stirred his tea bag round and squeezed the dark juice out of it. After adding some milk and sugar, he settled at the kitchen table, grabbed a handful of biscuits and waited for Fred to return. Whether he liked it or not, the ball was rolling and there was no way of stopping it. To his relief when Fred got back, he seemed in a much better temper.

"Okay, that's done, now we wait." Fred made himself a mug of tea and joined Bill at the table. "Tomorrow night I'll ring them, they should have the letter by then, but for now we stay put and keep a low profile."

Bill didn't answer; he nursed his mug of tea and stared moodily into its murky depths. The thought of spending hours cooped up with Fred didn't exactly thrill him. "I'm going upstairs, I need some sleep."

Fred just grunted a reply and continued stirring the sugar round in his mug.

Wearily, Bill climbed the stairs and made his way along the dark passage to one of the other bedrooms. On the floor were a couple of pump up beds, Bill lay on one; he hadn't realized how tired he was. He was soon asleep, snoring loudly.

Chapter 16

Alice rose early as sleep had eluded her. The whole night anxious thoughts about Tom had troubled her mind. *Where was he...was he safe?* Wearily, she carried a tray of tea upstairs to Ben and Amy.

There was a muffled response to her light tap on their door.

"I'll leave the tea out here," she said placing the tray on a small hall table. As she made her way to the kitchen, the postman arrived. There were a few bills, some magazines and a grubby brown envelope. Alice felt queasy as she held it, her hand shook—she knew it was from the kidnappers.

Sergeant Buoyed was sitting at the kitchen table drinking coffee. He looked up and could tell by the fearful expression on her face—the ransom note had arrived. He tried to look reassuring as he took the envelope from her and tore it open.

Alice hovered anxiously by the table

watching as he smoothed the crumpled paper and began to read. Her hands trembled as she twisted her apron. "Is it from them?" her voice faltered as she spoke.

"Yes, I am afraid it is. Can you go and fetch the Lewis's, while I ring Inspector Mullins?"

Alice climbed the stairs with a heavy heart. Outside the Lewis's bedroom door, she paused for a moment. Close to tears she took a few deep breaths. *I must stay calm, Mrs Lewis needs me.* The desire to weep was overwhelming.

Amy answered her gentle tap on the door, she sounded tired. "What is it Alice, is there some news?"

Alice fought to suppress her tears. "Yes, there is Mrs Lewis; the Sergeant would like you both to come to the kitchen."

There was a brief silence; when Amy spoke again her voice quivered.

"Okay, tell the officer we won't be a moment."

Alice could tell she was struggling to stay calm. She heard them talking softly as she turned and made her way downstairs.

The Sergeant looked up as she walked into the kitchen.

"They'll be here in a moment." She hovered anxiously by the kitchen table, her eyes glued to the crumpled letter.

"Good, I've managed to get hold of the Inspector and he's on his way."

Ben and Amy walked into the kitchen; they were agitated and full of questions. Amy hung onto Ben's arm for support. They both looked exhausted.

Alice could tell Amy had been crying, her eyes were puffy and red.

"What's happened?" asked Ben. "Have the kidnappers been in touch?"

"Yes, they have Mr Lewis. The ransom note just arrived, but there's nothing we can do until my D.I gets here."

As if on cue the door bell rang.

Alice shot to her feet and almost ran to let him in.

Mullins followed her into the kitchen, his facial expression grim. He didn't say a word; he took the letter from the Sergeant. When he'd finished reading it, he placed it on the table and gazed around at their anxious faces.

Ben frowned, his eyes darkened with anger and his hands shook. "So, do they have our son and what do they want?"

"They don't say a lot sir, but if I'm to believe this letter. They have Tom and they want two hundred thousand pounds for his safe return."

The room was filled with varying sounds of shock, as each person struggled to come to terms with what they were hearing.

In as gentle a tone as possible, Mullins continued. "In the letter they say they'll be in touch by phone this evening. Whoever these people are, they're definitely amateurs. I would say opportunists and I'm confident we'll get them." He picked up the letter and read it again.

Ben and Amy watched him, curious at his

puzzled expression. "What is it? What's the matter?" asked Ben.

Mullins put the letter down and stared at them his expression confused and questioning. "It says here that the boy has a rat with him, what on earth do they mean by that?"

Amy gasped; she could feel the colour drain from her face. She and Alice shot to their feet and ran up to Tom's room, followed by the others.

"Mask!" they called as they ran to the cage, but no response, the cage was empty.

"She's not here," cried Amy "They really do have Tom. There's no other way they could know about his rat?"

"Rat!" exclaimed Mullins. Confused he stared at the two women.

"Yes, Tom has a pet rat." Alice explained.

Amy clutched Ben's hand. "Oh God, Ben, she must be with Tom, how else would they know about his rat?"

"I have no idea sweetheart." He tried to comfort her, but his own heart was gripped with fear. He put his arm round her as they slowly filed downstairs to the kitchen.

They sat around the table, each one wrestling with their own thoughts and fears.

Tears trickled down Amy's cheeks.

Mullins reached across the table and gently touched her hand. "I know it's hard Mrs Lewis, but try not to worry."

"How can I not worry? They have my son!" She exclaimed. She leaned against Ben and wept openly.

"Yes, they have Mrs Lewis, but please, trust me. Once your phone is tapped; I guarantee when the call comes, we will trace it. I promise you, we'll find Tom and bring him home." He smiled reassuringly at her and turned to Ben. "Can I have a word with you sir?"

Ben rose from the table and followed him into the hall.

"I didn't want to discuss this in front of your wife, Mr Lewis. But I suggest you go to the bank and make arrangements. It's a large amount of money and could take some time to sort out. But don't worry you won't be paying the kidnappers, call it an insurance policy. Sergeant Buoyed will go with you."

Ben's face was grim and determined as he put his coat on. "I'll pay whatever they want, if it means we get Tom home safe and unharmed."

"Don't you worry sir, we'll get him back." Mullins expression was equally determined.

Chapter 17

Tom forced himself to be brave as he followed the narrow muddy path. Once his eyes adjusted to the darkness, he was able to avoid the deep ruts and the many boulders that threatened to trip him. The eerie cry of an owl heightened his sense of fear and despair. The hairs on the back of his neck tingled as he stared with fearful eyes into the tree tops.

He put a hand inside his coat pocket and felt for Mask's warm body. "Don't you worry," he said softly. "We'll escape from this forest." Tom's whispered words of encouragement did little to boost his confidence. He knew they were lost; all he could do was keep following the path and pray it would lead them out of the forest. He pulled his jacket close and forced his tired legs to move. Hunger gnawed at his stomach. What he wouldn't give for one of Alice's cooked breakfasts.

A cold grey fog settled over the forest. The only way he could stay relatively warm was to keep moving. His clothes felt damp against his skin. He shivered and moaned with discomfort. Added to his distress, he had no idea if his captors were chasing him, or how close they might be. For a brief moment Tom stopped and looked around; as far as he could see it was wall to wall trees. In the grey mist, they looked strangely spooky. But at least he was able to see more clearly.

When he'd first entered the forest it was pitch black and the slightest sound had terrified him. Whether the haunting call of an owl or the constant rustle of shrubbery, as a deer—or who knows what else, moved unseen through the thick undergrowth. Even a leaf falling on his head, caused him to cry out in fear. He was tense and exhausted, he needed to rest.

He noticed a large boulder at the side of the path. He sat on it, grateful to take the weight off his feet. *I'll just sit here for a moment.* He wanted to remove his shoes, as the souls of his feet burned and he had a blister, but he knew if he did, he probably wouldn't get them on again.

Mask moved restlessly in his pocket, so he lifted her out and held her close. Her presence comforted him, even though worrying about her added to his stress. She sat on his shoulder, while he rummaged in his bag for her water bottle.

The soft swish of an owl's wings startled him. He grabbed Mask—ignoring her squeak of protest and placed her on his lap, concealing her with his jacket. "I'm sorry; it's not safe for you on my shoulder. You have to stay hidden."

He found her water bottle; there wasn't much left. He was thirsty himself and would have loved a drink. He held the bottle for her and watched enviously as she eagerly finished off the remaining drop. "We'll have to find more water and some food soon. You must be hungry—I'm starving!" Tom held her close, and couldn't help but smile as she ground her teeth with contentment.

He gazed around; the thick fog had dispersed, leaving behind a veil of mist. Fragile daylight flickered through the tree tops. The combination of mist and early morning light gave the forest a strangely mystical atmosphere.

Tom noticed a clump of dandelions growing near the boulder. He bent down picked a leaf and offered it to Mask. She gave it a tentative sniff. "Come on," he encouraged. "You love dandelions. I'm hungry, so you must be." He wiggled the leaf in front of her nose and to his relief she took it from him and started to eat hardly pausing for breath. "See, I knew you wanted it." He grinned as he watched her hold the leaf in her dexterous paws. He loved the way her whiskers twitched as she chewed. *At least I've found something to feed you. Now I need food and water for myself.*

When Mask finished eating, he put her back in his pocket, where she would be safe. This was a dangerous place and he feared a bird would swoop down and grab her. Or something else might frighten her and cause her to run away. Tom knew whenever she was scared; she always ran to him. But in this alien environment he could not be sure how she would react. The thought of her being lost or hurt was too much to bear. He put his hand inside the pocket and stroked her. He smiled as she nibbled his finger nail. "You can't still be hungry Mask. At least you've had something to eat. I wish I could eat dandelion leaves."

He sat on the boulder listening to his rumbling tummy and fantasizing about one of Alice's delicious roast dinners—suddenly he remembered his mobile phone. He could have kicked himself. "Why didn't I think about it before?" He grabbed the bag and frantically searched through it. "I hope you haven't chewed it Mask." To his relief he found it at the bottom of the bag among his school books, his heart raced with excitement and hope. He held the precious phone in his hand. He couldn't wait to hear his father's voice.

He had no idea where he was, but he was confident his parents would find him. He switched the phone on—his heart sank. "Oh no," he groaned. "I don't believe it! The battery's dead and there's no signal." Hoping for a miracle, he got to his feet and standing on his toes, he held the phone high above his head. He turned it this way and that; in the desperate search for a signal, but to no avail. As a last resort, he climbed onto the boulder, but the dense forest of trees formed an impenetrable barrier.

"Stupid flipping thing," he shouted as he jumped to the ground. "You're useless; I wish Mask had chewed you!" Tears of frustration welled in his eyes; he brushed them away. He was so angry he could hardly contain himself. He walked to the edge of the path and threw the phone as hard as he could into the trees. He heard it smash as it hit something in the undergrowth. He thought the phones destruction would make him feel better...it didn't. Miserable, he slumped back onto the rock and cradled his head in his hands rocking back and forth in despair.

Mask stirred restlessly in his pocket.

Tom managed to pull himself together. He wiped his eyes and took a few deep breaths. "It's okay Mask." He put his hand over the pocket to calm her.

Gazing into the leafy canopy above his head, he prayed quietly. *Maybe there's another path, or a short cut out of this forest.* He latched onto the thought and gazed around hopefully. But as far as he could see there was no other path, just the one they were on. There were a few small tracks, but instinct told him they led nowhere. He grabbed his bag and started walking, continuing to pray quietly under his breath.

After he'd walked for some time, he looked at his watch, it was just after eleven. He felt weak with hunger, his tummy rumbled constantly. He wasn't sure how much further he could go. On the other side of the path he saw a mound of tufted grass, it looked welcoming. *It won't hurt to rest for a while.* Weary he lowered himself onto the soft grass. *I wish I could have a drink, I'm so thirsty.* He sighed, and for a moment rested his head in his hands and that's when he heard it...the sound of trickling water. He looked at the ground; it was wet where the water seeped across the path.

Trembling with excitement, Tom jumped to his feet and forced his way through the dense shrubbery searching for the source of the water. The further he pushed into the undergrowth, the soggier it became underfoot. Thirst drove him on. Determined not to give up, he struggled through the bushes and eventually found himself in a tiny clearing. And there it was, a small stream of clear water flowing over rocks and disappearing among the trees.

Overjoyed he fell to his knees and scooped the cool water into his hands. The thought it might not be safe to drink didn't even occur to him. He was so thirsty, he gulped the water; the coldness took his breath away. Once his thirst was quenched, he splashed the water over his face, it revived him. Then he took Mask's water bottle from his bag and filled it. "This should keep you going till we get help. I wish I had a bottle I could fill. "

Tom got to his feet and fought his way back to the main path. He felt refreshed, even his hunger pangs had eased. His feet still hurt, but revived by the water his pace quickened. As he walked along he thanked God for the stream of cool water. His situation had not changed, but somehow he didn't feel so alone. He knew his family would be praying and trying to find him; this thought gave him the courage he needed to keep going.

He felt Mask move inside his jacket and

grinned. He guessed she was probably chewing holes in the lining of his pocket, but he didn't care, he wasn't bothered about a few holes. As far as he was concerned she could chew the whole jacket if she wished. She'd helped him escape from the kidnappers. Because of her, he was free. He put his hand inside the pocket; she was settling down, but stirred as he touched her.

"Thanks Mask," he whispered. Tom knew without her he would still be tied to the chair in that dark dingy room. He shuddered at the thought and for a moment stopped and looked back. He was alone, no one followed him.

He hurried on, walking as fast as he could. Hours past and he was beginning to think he would never escape from the forest. It seemed to go on for ever. He was thirsty again and his stomach grumbled with hunger, but he forced himself to keep moving. Wearily he placed one foot in front of the other, hardly noticing the forest of trees around him. His thoughts were of home, of something hot to eat and his bed.

However, the further he went along the path it slowly dawned on him, the vast forest of trees appeared to be thinning out. To his relief he realized he was close to emerging from the darkness of the forest and into the light.

Chapter 18

Sure enough, a hundred yards or so in front of him, Tom could see green fields bathed in autumn sunshine. He grinned, never was a sight more welcome. "We've made it Mask, we've escaped from this horrible forest."

The sun's rays drew him on, filling him with hope. His heart skipped with excitement. He wanted to run but his legs were too tired. As he emerged from the darkness of the forest, he was forced to shield his eyes against the suns glare. Once they adjusted, he gazed around hoping to see a house or a farm. But everywhere he looked, it was just fields, hedgerows, and more forest.

Tom's face crumpled with disappointment. He walked into the sun and slumped in a tired heap on the grass. He needed to rest. He lifted Mask out of his pocket. "I bet you're thirsty? Do you want a drink?" He watched enviously as she readily accepted the cool stream water he'd collected earlier. When she finished he put the bottle away and held her close. "Which way do you think we should go? I wish you could tell me."

There were not many hours of daylight left and Tom knew he wouldn't survive another night in the open, with no food or shelter. As it was, he was weak with hunger. Suddenly, he remembered the chocolate in his pocket. It wasn't a lot, just a few squares, but it would give him some much needed energy.

He put Mask on his shoulder and fished in his pocket for the chocolate. Having been there some time it was coated in a whitish bloom, along with bits of fluff and a hair or two. But that didn't bother Tom; he cleaned it up...bit off a small piece for Mask, and rammed the rest in his mouth. He was so hungry; it was the best chocolate he'd ever tasted. He grinned as he watched Mask nibble her tiny piece. "Is that good?" His mouth was so full of melting chocolate, he could hardly talk.

Mask finished the last crumb and carefully washed her chocolaty paws, like Tom, she wasn't going to waste a bit.

"I don't know about you Mask? But I could do with a drink. I wish the stream was near." He stroked her and gazed around for any sign of life. Shielding his eyes against the glare of the sun, he noticed something in the distance. He couldn't be sure, but it looked like the roof of a building. It was hard to see through the trees, which was probably why he hadn't noticed it before.

Quickly, he put Mask in his pocket and

scrambled to his feet. Now he was standing, he could see it more clearly. "Wow, I think I can see a farm." His voice heightened with excitement. "I'm going to take a look." He forgot how tired he was and almost ran in his eagerness to get there. As he drew closer, he could see it was a farm. "Oh brilliant, now we can get help and Dad will come and fetch us." He pushed through a hedge and found himself on a rough cart track a few yards from an old barn.

He stood transfixed, hardly able to breathe or move. There in front of him, in all its run down glory was the dilapidated old farm house. The path through the forest had brought him full circle. It was the same farm he'd escaped from. Tom was devastated; a cold clammy sweat gripped him. For a moment he stood rooted to the spot, trembling and drained of energy. It was as though the house mocked him.

Tears of frustration trickled down his cheeks. His muscles froze with fear. *Oh God, I hope they haven't seen me, I have to hide.* He forced his leaden legs to move and stumbled towards the barn. He needed to keep out of sight and get his jumbled thoughts together.

He pushed the old barn door...close to falling off its rusty hinges it creaked and groaned as it opened. Tom shot a nervous glance towards the house, but there was no sign of life. He checked his watch, it was nearly three o'clock and already it was beginning to feel cold. Inside the barn there were a few straw bales and some rusty old farming equipment. The building itself was full of holes and looked as though a strong wind would bring it crashing to the ground.

At least it will be warmer in here, warmer than outside anyway. And I don't think those men know we're here. He sighed with relief. It occurred to him that if he was careful, he just might have an advantage over the kidnappers. As his tension eased, he smiled. *They have no idea I'm right under their noses.* The thought pleased him, but he knew he needed to be as quiet as possible; he dare not alert them to his presence.

Tom dropped his bag to the ground and slumped exhausted onto a bale of hay...glad to rest his legs. He lifted Mask from his pocket and put her on his shoulder. He smiled as she nibbled his finger. "You're hungry aren't you? So am I, but I've no food. There's some water though—here have a drink." He held the bottle, and as she drank he told her his plan. "In a while, when it's dark I'm going to try and get into the house," he whispered. "I don't see a car, so maybe they're out, probably looking for us." He grinned.

Having a modicum of control over his situation filled him with confidence and hope. "If there's a phone in the house, I'll ring my dad and he'll come and fetch us." His tummy rumbled a reminder of his hunger. "Maybe they'll have some food in there. I hope so, I'm starving."

He lifted her off his shoulder and gave her a gentle squeeze. "I'm so glad you're with me Mask." Thinking she might enjoy some freedom. Tom put her beside him on the bale of hay.

She stayed close to him, tentatively

nibbling the hay. The unfamiliar environment made her nervous.

"No, Mask, don't eat the hay, you'll be ill. It's damp and rotten." Tom lifted her onto his knees.

As they sat in the relative silence, faint scuffling sounds could be heard coming from the far corner of the building.

Mask froze, her ears twitched as she listened.

Aware she was nervous. Tom placed his hands around her in case she ran away. He looked across to where the sound came from. *I wonder what it is*. He decided it must be something bad as Mask seemed highly agitated. Her long tail twitched like a snake...not something Tom had ever seen her do before. He held his breath—his heart pounded. Tense and afraid to move, he listened to the scratching and rustling.

As he stared in the direction of the sound, he was horrified to see three large wild rats creep out from behind a piece of rusty farm equipment. Tom's eyes widened with fear as he watched them forage around in the hay. He clamped a trembling hand over his mouth...too late to stifle his fearful gasp—the rats heard him.

Alerted to his presence, they froze, fixing him with dark piercing eyes. The largest of the three swished his tail and fluffed his fur, increasing his size dramatically. The big rat's nose twitched as he sniffed the air.

Oh no, I bet it can smell Mask. Tom held onto her, sensing she was about to panic and do a runner. She squeaked and squirmed as he tried to put her in his pocket.

The wild rats began to show interest and moved a bit closer.

Tom shuddered as he watched them approach. Mask continued to squirm in his hands, refusing to go in the pocket. "Stop it, Mask! Get in there. I have to keep you safe." Though hushed, his voice rang with fear and frustration. His heart pounded—his hands trembled, but he managed to push her in.

Once she was in the pocket, the old familiar smell calmed her.

Relieved, Tom leapt to his feet and jumped onto the bale of hay.

His quick movement scared the rats, but only briefly. They quickly regrouped; their beady eyes glistened in the dim light as they watched him.

The higher vantage point made Tom feel safer and gave him a little confidence. Suppressing the desire to shout, he waved his arms and hissed to emphasise the point. It was ineffective, but he dare not make any loud noises. In desperation he stamped his foot, but the bale of hay muffled the sound. For a brief moment his frantic gesturing scared them and they scuttled away, but not far enough. In fact Tom was horrified to see more rats creep out and join the first three. Now, he really was afraid, but he knew if he raised his voice, the men would hear him.

Tom desperately looked around for something he could use as a weapon. He noticed a large piece of wood lying on the ground near to him. Without hesitation, he left the bale, grabbed the wood and threw it as hard as he could at the rats. They scattered like brown blurs and disappeared with loud squeaks of protest.

He took his chance and made a dash for the door. Once outside, he stood for a moment gasping for breath. His legs trembled violently and his tongue stuck to the roof of his mouth. He leaned against the door and took a few deep breaths, he needed to calm down. Putting a trembling hand in his jacket pocket, he felt for Mask. "You're not like them," he whispered.

Gently she licked his finger, enjoying the remains of melted chocolate stuck to his skin.

"We can't stay in there anymore. Not with wild rats about. When it's dark, they'll come back and I won't be able to see them." He shuddered at the thought. He'd never been close to a wild rat before. He could still see their narrow pointed faces and dark beady eyes. Now, he could understand why his mother feared them so much.

He ducked into the shadow of the barn and looked towards the house. As far as he could see there was no one around. He shivered and pulled his jacket close. *I can't stay out here, it's freezing and I need to find a phone.* Cautiously, he moved away from the barn, crouched low and crept towards the house. He could see no sign of a car, or any activity from inside the building. *Maybe they're not in there.* But he knew he must be careful, they could be anywhere. They could even be watching him.

Chapter 19

Tom held his breath as he snuck around the back of the house, it was quiet. He approached a small grubby window and peered in. The glass was so dirty he couldn't see much. He moved to the door and tried the handle, to his relief it opened. It took a second for his eyes to adjust in the dim light.

He looked around; apart from a table and a couple of chairs, the room was empty. A dripping tap reminded him he was thirsty. Taut with fear, but desperate for a drink, he moved towards the sink and turned the tap just enough for the slow drip to become a trickle. His need for water outweighed his fear of the men. He put his lips under the tap and gratefully swallowed the cool water. His thirst quenched and aware the sound of running water might be heard. He turned off the tap and backed into the shadows. He listened for footsteps...all he heard was his beating heart.

From his hiding place, he gazed wide eyed

at the table and stifled a delighted gasp. His mouth watered, as he looked at the large loaf of bread and packet of digestive biscuits. Famished, he rushed to the table and grabbed a few slices of the bread. He tore off a bit of crust for Mask.

She snatched it from him almost before his hand reached the pocket.

"Watch it Mask," he hissed. "You nearly had my fingers. I guess you're as hungry as me." He grinned and stuffed the remaining bread in his mouth; there was so much he could hardly chew. He put a couple of the biscuits in his trouser pocket for later.

For a moment he stood still—listening. But apart from the creaks and groans of the house, all was quiet. He held his breath as he crept out of the kitchen and made his way cautiously into the hall. He stayed in the shadows waiting for his eyes to adjust. Facing him was the front door and to the right of that another door...slightly ajar. Pale light from the room filtered into the hallway.

His stomach knotted and he hardly dare breathe as he made his way towards the door. The floorboards creaked alarmingly. He stopped and listened, his heart pounded. The bread he'd swallowed so fast, threatened to reappear. He groaned and clutched his stomach. *I must be quiet; if they're in the house they'll hear me.* Once his stomach settled, he inched slowly along the passage towards the door; it creaked slightly as he pushed it open. He grimaced and shot a nervous glance behind him. But there was no one there. He breathed a sigh of relief.

Tom stepped into the room and was instantly assailed by the chill air and musty damp smell. He shivered and screwed up his nose. He hated the house and couldn't wait to get away. But the need to find a phone gave him the courage to persevere. *There must be one in here somewhere—but where!*

Desperately, he searched the room, all the while praying under his breath. He noticed a laptop on the table in the far corner, and walked over to it. Beside the laptop was a mobile phone. With a sigh of relief, Tom grabbed it. *Great, thank you God. I hope it works.* He moved quickly into the shadows and flipped it open. He could have cried with joy, there was a signal. With trembling hands, he punched in his home number. It rang and rang. "Please be there," he whispered. Suddenly, he heard his mother's voice.

"Who is this?" she asked. She sounded strained and tearful.

Tom struggled hard to control his emotions. "Mother, it's me, Tom. Can you hear me?" he was whispering for fear of being heard by the kidnappers. He crouched down in the darkness.

"Oh my God, Tom, is it really you?" She burst into tears—then silence.

"Mother, are you there?" he whispered anxiously.

But his father answered. "Tom, its dad, where are you son, are you okay?"

Hearing his father's voice was too much for Tom, he began to cry.

Ben tried to calm him. "Don't cry son, listen to me. This call is being traced, but it takes time. Tell me, are you in a town; is it farmland or woods? Think, Tom, please!" Ben could hardly hide his desperation, as he waited for Tom to answer.

Tom managed to pull himself together. "It's a farm dad, really old and falling down. There are no other houses around. I escaped and walked through a huge forest, but it brought me back here. So I crept in and found this phone. Please, help me dad. I'm so scared."

"Stay calm Tom. We're coming to get you. Is Mask with you?"

"Yes, she was brilliant dad. She chewed through the ropes and set me free. Please hurry and get us."

"Don't you worry son, we're on our way."

Tom's hand shook as he gripped the phone. He could hear his father talking to someone. He was asking them about a trace, but Tom couldn't hear their reply. As he crouched there, waiting for his father to speak ... a hand grabbed him roughly by the collar. "Ahh!" he cried. "Let go of—" He dropped the phone and tried to kick the tall man hanging onto the collar of his jacket. "Dad, help me," he screamed. He could hear his father's muffled voice shouting. "Tom! Tom!"

Fred dragged him away by his collar, and forced him into a chair. "Watch him." He growled at Bill. He grinned as he picked up the phone. "You're just the man I need to talk to."

Ben was frantic. "Where's my son?" he

yelled down the phone. "You lay a finger on him and I'll—"

"Now then, let's keep calm." There was a mocking and sinister edge to Fred's voice. "Your boy's fine. We lost him briefly, but now he's safely back here with us. And he'll remain safe, just so long as you give us the money. Have you got it?"

The menacing tone in his voice unnerved Ben. Realising the danger Tom was in, he calmed himself. "Yes I have, but if you harm my son—"

Fred ignored him and grinned with satisfaction. He quickly explained where he wanted the money to be dropped. "Once we have it. I'll tell you where your kid is." He switched off the phone and turned to Bill. "Take him up to the room and lock him in. And this time make sure he can't escape."

Tom fought and kicked, but Bill held him firmly by the arm, and all but dragged him up the stairs to the dingy little room.

"My dad will find me," Tom shouted. "And when he does, you'll be—"

"Yeh, yeh, I'm sure." Bill laughed as he dragged him along the corridor.

"He will!" Tom shouted defiantly.

Bill pushed him into the room. "You stay in there kid, and behave yourself if you know what's good for you." He closed and bolted the door. This time the window was secure. There would be no escape.

Left alone, Tom perched nervously on the edge of the bed. As he stared around the dingy room, he swiftly grasped the reality of his situation—he was in danger. Trembling with fear, he wiped his clammy hands on his trousers. His whole body felt as though it was burning up. He clenched his fists and fought the overwhelming desire to panic. *I wonder if dad's managed to find out where I am. Oh God, I hope so.*

He felt Mask stir in his pocket. With trembling hands he lifted her out and put her on the bed.

She was glad to stretch her legs and her playful antics brought the faintest glimmer of a smile to his face.

Her presence comforted him. "Dad will come and get us soon, don't you worry." Tom prayed his words would prove to be true.

Unconcerned, Mask enjoyed her freedom, and the chance to explore. But once her curiosity was satisfied, she settled beside Tom and chewed holes in the grubby blanket.

As Tom stroked her, he remembered the digestive biscuits in his pocket. It was one of her favourite treats. He took a bite from one and gave her a bit. He was hungry, but a sudden wave of nausea took away his appetite for the biscuit. He shivered and pulled his jacket close. The house was eerily quiet. The only sound...Mask crunching on her biscuit.

Chapter 20

Ben slammed the phone down. His low growl of rage and clenched fists worried Amy. She'd never seen him like this before.

"Please, Ben, you're frightening me." She held onto his hand.

Ben took a few calming breaths and put his arm round her. There was nothing he could say, or do. The situation was completely out of his control. He felt powerless and frustrated.

"I heard a cry, was it really Tom?" Amy's voice broke as she struggled to keep her emotions in check.

Ben could feel her trembling. "Yes, it was. I just pray I was on the phone long enough for the police to get a trace."

Amy could hear the concern in his voice. She gazed up at him, he looked tired and pale.

Just then, D.I Mullins entered the room.

Tense with anticipation, Ben and Amy watched him approach.

As Mullins walked towards them, Ben

couldn't help but notice the optimistic glint in his eyes.

"Was it successful?" he asked eagerly. "Did they get a trace?" He prayed the answer was yes.

Not sure what to think, Amy looked from one to the other, trying to read their expressions. She turned to Mullins. "Please, tell us the trace was successful and you know where Tom is."

Mullins grinned triumphantly; he was relieved to be the bearer of good news. "Yes, Mrs Lewis we've managed to trace the call, and we know where your son is being held."

"Oh, thank God. That's wonderful." Amy clutched Ben's arm, her face a picture of relief and hope.

"Come, I'll show you where he is on this map."

As they followed him to the coffee table, Alice joined them, her eyes puffy from crying.

Mullins opened a large map and smoothed it out. "This is where he is. As you can see it's a vast area of forest and farmland, with very few buildings." He moved his finger over the map. "This derelict old farm is where they're holding Tom. The farm can only be approached by one narrow lane, but this actually works in our favour."

"Why?" asked Amy. Her eyes were glued to the map as if willing Tom to rise from the paper.

"We can block the lane," said Mullins. "The only way they'll escape, is on foot, or across the fields in a four by four. But from a witness account we know they don't have one of those." He gazed round at them. They looked pale and exhausted, but Mullins was pleased to see a flicker of hope in their eyes. He grinned with confidence...trust me...we've got them." He turned the map slightly and used his finger to point out a dark mass. "You see this part of the forest?"

They nodded and moved closer to peer at the map.

"Well, that's where your son was walking. The nearest village is a good twelve miles from the farm, on the other side of this forest. A boy of Tom's age would never have made it, especially not alone and in the dark."

Amy stared at Mullins with desperate eyes. "Are you sure he's at this farm?" Her voice faltered. Alice took her hand and gave it a comforting squeeze.

Mullins smiled reassuringly. "Oh yes! The signal definitely came from the farm. So don't you worry, we'll get him back." He folded the map and turned to Ben, a concerned frown creased his brow. "Mr Lewis, where did the kidnapper tell you to leave the money and did he give you a time?"

Ben nodded. "He told me to drop it by the side gate of Tom's school, behind the dustbins at nine o'clock tonight."

Instinctively every one looked at their watches.

"Good," said Mullins with a relieved smile. He studied his watch. "It's just after five now, so we have plenty of time to get to the farm before one of them leaves to pick up the money. We'll get Tom and arrest them both."

Amy gasped. "How do you know there's more than one?"

"Past experience Mrs Lewis, you rarely get just one kidnapper." He turned and hurried into the hall. "Excuse me for one moment; I need to make some calls." His voice rang with urgency as he barked orders into his phone. "I want two unmarked cars...extra police officers, a marksman and an ambulance, and I need them now!"

Amy and Alice gave each other nervous glances. They realised the situation was coming to a head, heightening their concern for Tom.

Ben gave Alice a reassuring pat on the shoulder.

Amy gazed into his face, her eyes puffy...her expression troubled.

Ben brushed a strand of hair away from her forehead. She looked so pale and drawn. He pulled her close.

"What if something goes wrong Ben? There will be armed police and you know how I hate guns."

"Try not to worry sweetheart, everything's going to be fine. Come and sit down...you too Alice." He led them to the couch—they both looked pale and anxious as they huddled together.

Alice's stomach churned with anxiety. Tom was like a son to her, but for Amy's sake, she did her best to hide her concern. Keeping everyone fed and watered was her way of coping.

Gently, she took Amy's hand—it felt cold. "We will get Tom home safely. I know we will."

Deep inside Amy believed her.

The two women clung to each other, their eyes glued to Ben.

How he wished he could do, or say, something to reassure them. He hated feeling out of control. He was a decision maker, a business man, used to being in charge—giving orders, but he had no answers. He could do nothing, but pray, and trust the police to bring the situation to a successful conclusion. The struggle to control his emotions and desperate concern for Tom exhausted him. But he needed to stay strong for Amy and Alice, they were depending on him.

Desperate for reassurance, Amy's eyes never left his face. "They will find him Ben— won't they? They will get him away from those awful men?"

"Yes, I believe they will. We have to keep faith sweetheart and be strong. I believe everything will go according to plan. Our son will be home with us soon... safe and well." He felt his faith rise as he spoke the words. A fragile sense of hope took root deep in his spirit. He took Amy's hand and said a silent prayer.

Alice put a comforting arm round her.

Mullins stood in the doorway and knocked gently. "Okay Mr Lewis, I'm sorry to disturb you, but we have to make a move. You will have to stay here Mrs Lewis."

Amy stood to protest. "No, please, I need to—"

Gently, Alice took her by the arm and

135

drew her back onto the couch.

"He's right Amy," said Ben. "You must stay here with Alice. It would be way too dangerous for you to come with us. As soon as we have Tom, I'll ring you, I promise." He leaned over and gently kissed her. "Look after her Alice."

"I will sir."

A worried frown darkened Ben's features as he strode with Mullins to the waiting cars.

Amy and Alice huddled together, holding hands for comfort.

They could hear the gravel crunch under the wheels of the cars as they pulled away from the house.

Their tearful prayers broke the ensuing silence.

Chapter 21

It was just after seven thirty when the police convoy arrived at the farm. They parked at the end of the drive, out of sight of the house. For a brief moment there was hectic, but silent activity as officers took up their positions.

The marksmen picked a spot near the barn, as close to the house as he could safely get. Other officers surrounded the farm house. A car had been placed across the drive, to prevent any escape by road.

Mullins and Ben stayed by the cars. They could only hope the kidnappers were still in the building.

Mullins used his binoculars to check out the house. "I can see a light in a downstairs room, but there's no sign of movement."

"So what happens now?" asked Ben.

"We wait, and keep in touch by radio. Once every one's in position we'll give it awhile and then attempt to enter the house. It's a tricky situation; we don't want any harm to come to

137

Tom. This is a—" He was about to continue when his radio burst into life.

It was the marksman. Through his high powered telescopic lens he was able to see inside the house. "There's no sign of the boy," he whispered into his radio. "But I can see one of the kidnappers".

"Don't do anything, just watch" Mullins told him. "But let me know if you see any more adults."

Ben struggled to keep his nerves under control; he hoped and prayed this marksman was not trigger happy. He ran a trembling hand through his hair. He could hardly swallow his mouth was so dry.

The radio burst into life again, this time an officer told them he'd found the kidnapper's car. "It's parked at the rear of the house," he said in a low voice.

"Good," said Mullins. "They're still here." Speaking softly into his radio, he instructed every one to lie low until he gave the word. It went quiet.

Ben desperately tried to keep calm. His mind reeled with thoughts of Tom. *Where were they keeping him? Was he alright*? His heart thumped in his chest— fearful thoughts crashed around in his head.

The silence was eerie, like the quiet before a storm. A fox barked in the distance disturbing the uneasy silence.

Ben pulled his coat tighter around him, there was a distinct chill in the air, but his palms were sticky with sweat. He wiped them on his coat. He was deep in thought when Mullins radio crackled into life again.

It was one of the officers. "I've positioned men near the doors and windows of the house," he told Mullins in a whisper. "The place is completely locked down; no one in that house is going anywhere."

Mullins grinned and switched the radio off—it went quiet. Every one held their positions and waited.

Ben shivered; he put his hands in his pockets and leaned against the police car. *How long is this going to take, I wonder*? He was cold...tired and desperately concerned for Tom and yet he felt strangely relaxed and confident.

All of a sudden a gunshot shattered the silence, followed by a loud cry from inside the house.

"Oh God—what was that?" Ben's heart leapt into his mouth.

D.I Mullins bellowed into his radio. "It's a Go, Go! Go!"

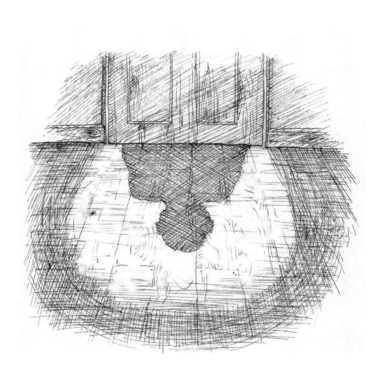

Chapter 22

Tom went to the window and gazed into the darkness. It was a moonless night; he could see nothing. He had no idea the police and his father were outside. But he felt sure he'd heard a noise, it was just too dark to see. He stood for a while listening, staring into the night sky, and praying he would soon be rescued.

He turned away from the window and stared into the dingy room. A faint glimmer of light came under the door from the hallway. Carefully Tom made his way to the bed. "Where are you Mask?" He tapped gently on the bed cover. Her cold nose touched his finger. "There you are." He scooped her up in his hands and held her close.

She stayed still, seeming to know how he felt...he needed her.

Tom sat on the edge of the bed stroking her; he gained comfort from her presence. All of a sudden, he heard heavy footsteps climbing the stairs. His heart leapt into his mouth. Quickly he put Mask inside his coat pocket...looked towards the door and waited. Sure enough as he watched, a dark shadow blocked the faint light coming under the door. He heard the clink of keys and a muttered curse. Tom shot to his feet, if there was any chance of escape; he would to be ready to take it.

The door opened and Bill's ample frame filled the space. "Okay kid, we want you downstairs." He stood aside to let Tom pass. "Don't even think about trying anything. My mate's not one to cross, so you behave yourself, do you hear?" To emphasise the point, he grabbed Tom's collar and ushered him down the creaky stairs into the front room. He pushed him towards the old armchair. "Sit there, where we can keep an eye on you, and don't move."

Tom perched on the chair and stared around. The dull glow from the naked light bulb swinging from the ceiling, made little impression on the dingy room. The furthest corners remained in shadow. The room was cold with a pervading musty smell. Tom shivered and struggled to suppress a sneeze. He gazed up at the cracked ceiling, noticing the many damp patches, and the liberal covering of cobwebs. They hung down like grubby grey curtains, the resident spiders long gone.

He turned his attention to Bill and Fred; they were huddled in a dark corner whispering to each other. Deep in conversation they seemed unaware of him. Slowly, he turned his head and looked towards the door. *This could be my chance to escape. While they're not looking, I'll make a run for it*. As quietly as he could he shifted to the edge of the chair, as his feet touched the floor he made to rise and bolt for the door.

"Don't even think about it!" growled Fred. "Move from that chair and see what happens."

Taken by surprise, Tom nearly jumped out of his skin. "You can't keep me here," he shouted, with as much courage and bravado as a nine year old could muster. "I want to go home. My father will find me, you'll see."

Furious, Fred spun round and glared at him.

Tom's heart raced with fear; nervously he chewed his bottom lip, but defiantly held Fred's gaze. As he stared into the man's cold dark eyes, he realised Bill's words were true. This was not a man to cross. Tom wished he could sink into the chair and hide.

Fred scowled and strode over to him. From his pocket he pulled a small hand gun, which he pointed at Tom's head.

Tom stifled a frightened cry and attempted to move further back in the chair, afraid even to breathe.

Having made his point, Fred put the gun away and leaned close to Tom's face.

Tom dropped his head and stared at his knees. Fred was so close he could smell the whisky on his breath.

"You will go home when we get our money and not before. Give us any trouble kid and you won't be going anywhere, do you understand me?"

Tom just nodded and kept his head low. When he looked up the two men were in the corner again, arguing.

"You didn't tell me you had a gun, how could you be so stupid, you're putting us in danger, we don't need a gun. We just get the money, release the kid and disappear." Bill's face was beetroot red with anger. His hands were balled into fists as he faced Fred.

The two men glared at each other.

Tom felt sure they would come to blows.

The atmosphere was so tense you could have cut it with a knife.

Trembling with fear, Tom put a shaky hand inside his jacket and felt for Mask, her presence soothed him. He was ready to escape the first chance he got. He watched the two men as they continued to argue.

"This is my insurance," Fred almost shouted, pulling the gun from his pocket and waving it around.

"Put that thing away before someone gets hurt." Bill struggled to keep his nerves under control. He knew the gun gave Fred an edge and he didn't like it. He was beginning to think he could end up penniless—or worse—a bullet in the back. To break the tension and hide his fear, he glanced at his watch. "When are you going for the cash?" He tried to keep his voice as normal as possible.

Fred's cold eyes creased in a sinister grin, he knew he had the advantage. He put the gun in his pocket and grabbed the car keys. "I'm leaving now," he snapped. He put his face close to Bill's, his expression dark and threatening. "You just make sure you watch him." He glared across at Tom. "If he gets away again, you're a dead man." He patted the gun in his pocket, his voice low and menacing.

Bill held his ground, as Fred straightened and walked away.

Tom cowered in the chair as he walked towards him.

"You stay put kid, or else." He reached down and grabbed hold of Tom by the front of his jacket, unaware he had hold of Mask as well.

She squeaked in pain. Her razor sharp teeth scythed through Tom's jacket and sank deep into his finger.

"Ouch! What the heck was that? Something bit me." He let go of Tom and clutched his bleeding finger cursing loudly.

In a split second Tom scrambled off the chair and made a run for the door.

"Stop him!" Fred yelled.

Taken by surprise at this turn of events, Bill stood transfixed as Fred went for the gun in his pocket and aimed it at the fleeing youngster.

Seeing the gun brought Bill to his senses. "No!" he bellowed and charged at Fred. He lunged and made a grab for the gun, they wrestled swearing and grunting.

Tom didn't stop or look around. He heard a loud bang... followed by a cry, but he kept going. Terrified he fled into the hall. He stood there shaking, not sure what to do, or where to go.

Abruptly and as if by magic, shouting

policemen seemed to appear from everywhere. One of them scooped him up, ran outside and placed him in the arms of another man.

Numb with fear, Tom clung to the man.

"Oh Tom, thank God you're okay."

Recognizing the voice, Tom pulled away and stared into the face of his father. "Dad, you're here."

Ben hugged and kissed him. "I've been here all the time Tom. Your mother and I have been out of our minds with worry." He brushed a strand of damp hair away from Tom's eyes. "You're okay now son, everything's going to be fine."

Tom sighed with contentment as he snuggled close to his father. He was safe—but so tired.

Ben held his son close and watched him sleep. The nightmare was over. A relieved smile erased the tension and worry from his face.

Chapter 23

Amy sat on the edge of Tom's bed and gently dabbed his forehead with a soft towel. The past week had been a nightmare. Watching her son battle with Pneumonia was not something she would easily forget. She fought back tears as she gazed at his young face...so pale and drawn. At least the tossing and turning had ceased and he was no longer moaning, crying out and throwing off his covers.

Ben stood at the end of the bed beside Doctor James. Though exhausted the relief was evident on his face.

Alice came into the room with a jug of ice-cold water. "How is he?" she whispered.

Tom stirred and tried to raise his head. "Mask" he moaned softly. For a second his eyes opened and he reached for his mother's hand.

Amy gently eased him back onto the pillow. "It's alright darling you rest." She stared at the Doctor, her facial expression concerned and questioning. "He keeps saying Mask, what does it mean? It's such a strange word."

"Perhaps he's had some sort of bad dream," suggested Alice as she placed the jug of water on the dresser.

The Doctor smiled reassuringly. "Yes, it's very possible, but Tom's going to be fine Mrs Lewis, you mustn't worry. The worst is over. The fever's broken now, he just needs to recuperate and gain strength. Make sure he drinks plenty of fluids and as soon as he's ready give him some solid food. This has been a nasty virus, but he's on the mend."

Alice gazed at Tom, her eyes filled with love and concern. "What an awful time this has been, but thank God our prayers have been answered." She smiled with relief.

"Yes, they have," said Amy. Gently she brushed a strand of damp hair away from Tom's forehead. She took his hand—it felt cold.

The Doctor gazed sympathetically at the three adults; they all looked so pale and tired, especially Amy, which was hardly surprising. "Trust me," he said softly. "Tom's going to be fine. Just do what I've said and he'll soon be up and about." He handed Ben a prescription. "Give him these and I'll pop in later in the week to check on him."

"Okay, thanks Doctor." Ben stared at his son, hardly able to express his relief.

"Now don't you worry Mr Lewis. Young Tom's given us all a bit of a fright, but he's on the mend now." The Doctor closed his bag and walked to the bedroom door.

"Let me show you out Doctor," said Alice

following him to the door.

"Thank you Alice, but there really is no need," he smiled. "I think I know the way by now, don't you?"

Muted laughter followed them as they made their way downstairs. "I'll be back in a few days Alice, to check on him."

"Thank you Doctor." She smiled and closed the front door.

Dr James put his medical case on the passenger seat of the car and eased in behind the wheel. Wearily, he leaned back in the seat. *This has been a tough few days, but thank God the child has recovered.* He smiled. *It's good to hear laughter in that house again.*

☙❧

Day by day Tom slowly recovered and gained strength. He was able to get up and about, but it would be a week or two before he was strong enough to return to school.

Amy was thrilled at his progress. He was well on the way to a complete recovery. But a slight concern niggled at the back of her mind. The word Mask was never far from his lips...each time he mentioned it, he would become strangely melancholy.

Amy sighed as she sat at the kitchen table nursing her coffee cup.

Alice sat opposite; she noticed Amy's pensive expression. "Is something bothering you Mrs Lewis?" she asked.

"I'm concerned about Tom, Alice.

Physically, he's doing well, but he's not himself, he seems so withdrawn. I know he's basically a quiet boy, but this is something else and I can't put my finger on it."

Alice frowned. "I know what you mean. It's as though he's had a bad dream, but can't quite remember it."

"Yes, and I'm sure it has something to do with that wretched word—Mask. It seems to haunt him. I wish I could help him...I feel so helpless. Do you think I should take him to the Doctor?"

Before Alice could answer, the back door flew open and Ben strode in carrying a large cardboard box. "Definitely, no Doctors," he said with a broad smile. "I think I have something here that will cheer him up. Where is he?"

Curious, Amy stared at her husband and the large box in his arms—it looked heavy. She rose from her chair. "What on earth have you got there?"

Ben grinned and backed away. "You'll see, where's Tom?"

"Up in his room, I think...reading."

Alice frowned slightly. "Please, don't think me rude Mr Lewis, but I don't think Tom needs anymore toys."

Ben grinned at her over the box, but made no comment. "Come on, both of you, follow me." He led the way, taking the stairs two at a time.

Amy and Alice gave each other curious glances as they followed him.

Tom lay on his bed staring up at the ceiling. He was bored with the book. He found it hard to concentrate on anything since recovering from his illness. Something constantly niggled at the back of his mind, but try as he might; he couldn't remember what it was, except for one word—Mask. Each time he thought of it, he felt strangely fearful. He would break out in a clammy sweat and struggle to breathe. The word haunted him and seemed to stir a powerful emotion within him.

Frustrated, he banged his fists on the bed. *I don't understand what is it? Who is it? I wish I could remember.* Tears pooled in his eyes, he suppressed them. A soft knock on the door made him jump.

"Tom, son, its dad, can I come in?"

Tom took a few calming breaths and propped himself up against the head-rest. "Yes Dad."

Slowly, the door opened and his father entered carrying a large box...followed by his mother and Alice. Their bemused expressions heightened Tom's curiosity. Intrigued he gazed from one to the other.

"I have something for you Tom, which I hope you'll like." Ben placed the box on the floor, lifted the flaps and pulled out a small white puppy. Gently, he placed the puppy on the bed and stood back.

Amy gasped with surprise. "You've bought him a dog!"

Ben smiled. "Yes, she's some sort of

terrier." He watched Tom with raised eyebrows, surprised at his reaction. He'd expected cries of delight, not tears.

Tom stared at the puppy, his eyes wide with shock and surprise. "Mask" he wailed. Deep sobs racked his body.

The puppy wagged its tail and waddled up to him.

He grabbed hold of her and held her close. His tears fell onto her soft fur.

Amy rushed to the bed and put her arms around him. "What is it darling? I don't understand." She stared into his tear stained face. "Tom, for so long you've pestered us for a dog. I would have thought you'd be delighted."

Ben frowned as he sat on the edge of the bed. "I'm sorry son; I thought it's what you wanted." He reached for the puppy, now snuggled in Tom's arms. "I'll take her back, don't worry."

Tom held on to her. "No! Dad, please don't take her. I love her. It's just that she reminds me of Mask." Tom sobbed again and his mother wrapped her arms round him.

"Oh, darling, what's the matter...who is this Mask?"

"She's a white rat," said Tom through his tears.

"What, a rat!" Amy gasped and almost drew back.

"Yes, a rat." Tom chewed nervously on his bottom lip. He knew how much his mother hated rodents. He could see the revulsion in her eyes. "I had an awful dream while I was ill and the rat saved me," he explained. "Seeing the puppy brought it all back. I don't remember everything, but I know you were all in it and a lady called Jean."

Ben exchanged a quick glance with Amy. "Why would you dream about Jean? You hardly know her, nor do we come to that."

"Isn't she the woman at church, who keeps rats?" Amy grimaced. "I believe she takes them to shows and stuff." She shuddered at the thought.

Ben nodded...his eyes glued to Tom. "Can you remember anything about the dream son?" He perched on the bed and stared into Tom's face.

Alice stood behind Amy, a concerned expression on her face. "From the state you're in Tom, I would say it was more of a nightmare."

Tom responded with a tearful nod. "It was, Alice, but I can't really remember much."

"Well, tell us what you do remember," said Ben.

Amy shot him a worried glance. "I'm not sure that's such a good idea."

"I know you're concerned Amy, but he needs to speak it out. We have to face our fears, because when we do, they lose the power to frighten us." He turned to Tom. "Tell us what you remember of the dream son. Don't be afraid, it can't hurt you."

Tom stared with panicked eyes into his father's face.

Ben smiled and nodded encouragement.

Tom held the puppy close and nervously

cleared his throat. "In the dream, I was locked in a dark room by two horrible men, but I managed to escape. But after that I got lost in a huge forest, I was so afraid."

"But where does the rat come into it, Tom?" Alice asked.

"I found the rat in our watering can, and I called her Mask. She helped me escape from the two men. They'd tied me to a chair and she chewed through the rope and set me free." He paused and stared at their concerned faces. Fresh tears fell as he stroked the puppy.

Amy took his hand. "Tom, your father's given you a puppy. I don't understand why that would that trigger memories of a nightmare."

Ben smiled slightly. "Yes, I must admit I'm intrigued myself. Tell me son, when you first saw the puppy, why did you call her Mask?"

Tom put his hand under the puppies chin and gently raised her head. "She has a black mask on her face, just like the rat in my dream." He fought back tears as he stroked the sleepy puppy.

Amy and Alice gasped with surprise.

"I don't like rats, but that's amazing."

"I know you don't like rat's Mum, but she was special."

"If you say so Tom," said Amy with a wry smile.

"She was." Tom insisted. "She saved me and I loved her. I thought she was real." Fresh tears fell. Tom's voice broke with emotion as he turned to his father. "When you put the puppy on the bed, I suddenly remembered bits of the dream. I know it wasn't real and I'm glad because it frightened me. But I wanted the rat to be real."

"Okay Tom, let's think of it this way. In your dream, Mask was a rat."

Tom nodded.

"Well, if you want my opinion, I think you were dreaming about this puppy. For the rat to have the same markings was no coincidence. I believe this is Mask," said Ben, picking up the sleepy pup.

Tom's face brightened and a little colour tinged his cheeks. "Yes, she is and I love her, thanks Dad. And I do feel better now I've told you the dream."

Ben affectionately tousled his hair. "Good, I knew you would." He smiled at Amy and gave her an '*I told you so look.*'

Amy grinned, but ignored him. She turned to Tom. "Why don't you take the puppy into the garden? It would do you good to get some fresh air."

Tom leapt off the bed. "Yes, come on Mask, let's go and play." He grabbed the puppy and dashed downstairs.

Alice laughed as she followed him. "Well, I'm glad that's all sorted. I'm going to make some lunch."

Ben and Amy smiled as they sat on Tom's bed and listened to his squeals of delight as he chased the yapping puppy around the garden.

Ben took Amy's hand. "You know, I've been thinking."

Amy grinned. "Careful."

"No, I'm serious," said Ben.

"So I see. What's troubling you?"

"I'm not troubled as such. It's Tom's nightmare. I think it's a wake-up call."

Amy stared into his face; he had that serious look she knew so well. "What do you mean—wake-up call?"

"I think I need to tighten the security around here. Not only that, we need to be more aware of Tom's safety." Ben noticed a flash of concern in Amy's eyes. He squeezed her hand. "It's okay, there's no need to worry."

"There is, if you think Tom could be in some sort of danger."

Ben frowned. "I don't think that at all. I'm just saying we need to be wise. It will do no harm to tighten security and make sure Tom is safe—you too for that matter." He could see a flicker of concern in her eyes and drew her close. "You're both precious to me," he said softly.

Amy smiled at him. "I do agree with you. It just worries me you're thinking like this. But I suppose you're right."

"Aren't I always," said Ben with a cheeky grin.

Amy gave him a derisive look and laughed. "No, I don't think so." She grabbed him by the hand and dragged him across to the window. They stood for a while watching Tom play with Mask. They'd never seen him so happy. For a brief moment he looked up at them and waved.

Ben and Amy waved back their faces wreathed in smiles.

"Just look at him Ben. I've never seen him like that. Thank you for getting him the puppy. I know we weren't keen on him having a pet, but I'm sure we'll manage and it's just what he needed."

"Yes, it is and I don't suppose one puppy will cause too much upheaval." He smiled and put his arm round her.

Amy leaned against him, resting her head on his shoulder.

Ben pulled her close and sighed. If he'd learned one thing during Tom's traumatic illness, it was how much his family meant to him. Seeing Tom well and happy was the icing on the cake.

Ben gazed heavenward and mouthed a silent prayer of thanks.

About the Author

Yvonne was born in Swindon Wiltshire, the eldest of three children.

From a young age her greatest joy, was to curl up with a good book. Over time she naturally progressed into writing. At the age of ten, she ambitiously attempted her first novel, but quickly gave up. However, the seed was planted. And in the coming years, in between a successful singing career, she continued to put pen to paper.

In recent years she has had short stories and articles published in the pet section of a national newspaper.

Her first book, The Shadowed Valley, was published in 2011.

45426624R00096

Printed in Poland
by Amazon Fulfillment
Poland Sp. z o.o., Wrocław